XA
FIC
14

COPY 2

Duncan, Lois, 1934-
Locked in time

AR Middle School RL: 6.5
Pts: 10.0

LOCKED IN TIME

Current Books by Lois Duncan

FICTION

Ransom
They Never Came Home
Hotel for Dogs
A Gift of Magic
I Know What You Did Last Summer
Down a Dark Hall
Summer of Fear
Killing Mr. Griffin
Daughters of Eve
Stranger with My Face
The Third Eye
Locked in Time

NONFICTION

How to Write and Sell Your Personal Experiences
Chapters: My Growth as a Writer

VERSE

From Spring to Spring
The Terrible Tales of Happy Days School

LOCKED IN TIME

Lois Duncan

Little, Brown and Company
BOSTON   TORONTO

FIRST EDITION

LIBRARY OF CONGRESS CATALOGING IN PUBLICATION DATA

Duncan, Lois, 1934–
Locked in time.

Summary: Nore arrives at her stepmother's Louisiana
plantation to find her new family odd and an aura of evil
and mystery about the place.
[1. Mystery and detective stories] I. Title.
PZ7.D9117Lo 1985   [Fic]   85-23
ISBN 0-316-19555-3

BP

Designed by Dede Cummings

Published simultaneously in Canada
by Little, Brown & Company (Canada) Limited

PRINTED IN THE UNITED STATES OF AMERICA

For my good friends
Don and Eileen Stanton

LOCKED
IN TIME

CHAPTER

1

W HEN I look in the mirror, the girl I see there is
pretty.

I know the statement sounds vain, but I hope it won't be
taken that way. When you're seventeen and a half, being
pretty comes with the territory. Smooth unlined skin, shiny
hair (mine is strawberry blond), trim hips, firm breasts —
that's what being young is all about. I know that I'm not
going to look this way indefinitely. Twenty-five years from
now, if I am lucky, people may refer to me as "interesting
looking." That's the best that I can hope for, and it will be
good enough.

But, at this special time in life, I'm pretty, and that makes
me happy. I certainly didn't feel that way, however, on that
day last June when my nightmare summer at Shadow Grove
began.

In many places, early June is considered summer, but that
is not always the way it is in New England. On that particular
morning, as I boarded the plane in Boston, it still seemed

like springtime, a fragile season of cool, sweet mornings and pale lemon sunlight. That was the last I was to see of that sort of weather. When, hours later, I descended the ramp at the airport in Baton Rouge, I felt as if I were walking into a steam bath.

The thick, damp heat rolled up to meet me, and I felt myself wilting on the spot. My hair, newly washed that morning, sagged limply against my neck, and drops of perspiration broke out on my upper lip. My face began to prickle the way it used to back when I was younger and preparing for an outbreak of acne. Before I got halfway down the steps, my sophisticated, high-necked blouse was glued to my skin like Saran Wrap.

Descending the ramp to the runway, I fell into step with the rest of the passengers who were streaming toward the terminal building. I did not see my father in the lineup of people waiting at the gate. Stepping through the door into the blessed air conditioning, I glanced worriedly about me. As angry as I was with him, it had never once occurred to me that he would not be there to meet me. Was it possible that he could have forgotten I was coming?

Before I had a chance to pursue that thought any further, Dad's strong hands grasped my shoulders. An instant later, I was spun around to face him and pulled tight against his chest in a crushing bear hug. The familiar scent of his aftershave filled my nostrils, and a sandpaper cheek ground hard against my forehead.

"Dad!" I exclaimed. "Oh, Daddy!"

I had meant to hold back — to act aloof and chilly — to let him know without doubt how absolutely furious I was. Instead, my arms flew up to encircle his neck.

"Daddy!" I cried, as though I were five years old again

and just home from kindergarten, bursting into his office to reassure myself that he had not vanished during my absence. "Oh, Daddy! I'm so glad to see you!"

"Nore, baby!" He released me from the hug and thrust me back at arm's length for a prolonged inspection. "God, you're so grown up! What have you done to yourself? This can't all have happened since last Christmas!"

"It didn't," I told him.

There was a moment of silence.

Then Dad said quietly, "I'm sorry, honey. I guess I wasn't noticing much of anything back last winter. I promise you, though, things are going to be different now." He changed the subject abruptly. "How was the flight? Are you hungry? Would you like to get something to eat before we head home? We've got an hour and a half's drive ahead of us, so if you're feeling empty, now's the time to do something about it."

"The flight was fine, and they served lunch on the plane." My eyes flicked nervously past him. "Did anybody come with you?"

"No, I came by myself," Dad said. "Lisette and the kids are dying to meet you, but Lis thought it would be best if you and I had some time alone together first. She knows that we've got a lot of catching up to do." He put his arm around my shoulders. "How many suitcases did you bring?"

"Only two," I said. "I had my winter things stored at the school."

"That was sensible," Dad said approvingly. "You're not going to need them here, and that's for sure. From what people tell me, by this time next month it's going to be hotter than Hades."

We collected the suitcases at the luggage claim, and I

5

waited with them at the pickup area in front of the terminal building while my father went to the parking lot to get the car. Alien sounds and sights and smells barraged my senses. A dark-skinned man had parked his pushcart in the center of the sidewalk and was selling a waferlike candy made of nuts and brown sugar. A woman in a flowing orange dress glided past me, carrying a basket of pale, waxen blossoms which I could not identify by name. I caught fragments of conversations held by voices with soft, strange accents that made the words sound almost like music. A couple next to me were speaking in French, and from somewhere behind me, a child's voice chattered excitedly in Spanish. Even the air smelled different, heavy and musky, rich with muted odors that I did not recognize.

The car that was inching its way toward me in the slow-moving line of traffic was familiar, however — far too familiar. It was the same tan station wagon that had once brought me home from Girl Scout meetings, from ballet lessons, from the skating rink, from the houses of middle school classmates. It was a car that belonged, not here in Louisiana, but back in Guilderland, New York, where I had spent the first fifteen years of my life.

The slanting, afternoon sunlight glinted off the windshield and rendered it opaque. My heart filled in the face that I longed to see behind it. The sweet mouth smiled. Clear, blue eyes squinted half closed against the sun. Unkempt brown curls, lightly threaded with silver, bounced against soft cheeks. I drew a ragged breath and averted my gaze.

The car kept moving forward and soon pulled up beside me. It was, of course, my father, and not my mother, who sat behind the wheel.

"Sorry to be so long, hon," he said apologetically. "The parking lot attendant gave me his whole life story while he counted out change. That's how it is in the Southland; the word 'hurry' isn't part of the vocabulary."

He got out of the car and went around to open the back. The latch was stuck, and he had to rattle it hard to get the tailgate down. For some perverse reason, that fact pleased me. The latch that had never worked easily for my mother would have had no business accommodating my father now. The memory of Mother, her arms filled with groceries, pounding the latch with her wristbone and struggling to keep from swearing, would have made me smile if the accompanying sense of loss had not been so painful.

I got into the car on the passenger's side. Dad eventually did get the back open and loaded in my suitcases. Then he shoved the door closed and came forward to climb into the driver's seat.

"So — off we go!" he said.

The jovial note in his voice was so at odds with my own emotions that I couldn't begin to respond to it. The drive would take us an hour and a half, he had told me. In just ninety minutes I would be meeting the woman who had taken my mother's place in my father's life.

We started off on the city freeway, but before many miles had been covered, Dad turned the car onto an exit ramp that led to a two-lane highway. This road was bracketed by shrubs and pine woods, and the sky beyond them gleamed with the odd iridescent sheen of sunlight being fed through a prism. Gazing out through the window beside me, I found myself experiencing the eerie sensation that nothing I was seeing was real. Veils of Spanish moss hung like gray crepe from the arching branches of oak trees, and clouds of large, black birds rose from nowhere with high-pitched cries and then sank down again into the foliage. Ahead of us, the asphalt shimmered as though spotted by puddles, but by the time we reached them, they had vanished and reappeared farther up the road.

For a long time we drove without speaking.

It was Dad who finally broke the silence.

"I know how surprised you must have been to get my letter. Shocked, even." When I did not respond, he continued, "I owe you an apology, Nore. I should have written sooner. The truth is, though, that there wasn't any 'sooner.' It all happened so fast."

"I guess it must have." I made no attempt to hide my bitterness. "One day you're a grieving widower, and the next, you're a bridegroom. That's fast, all right."

"I fell in love," Dad said simply.

"Mother hasn't even been gone a year yet!"

"Don't you think I know that?" Pain rose, sudden and fierce, in his voice. "The day your mother died was the most terrible of my life. I went through the next half year like a zombie. That's why I insisted that you go off to boarding school; I didn't want you to have to share a home with somebody in my condition. I couldn't eat without vomiting. I couldn't sleep for the nightmares. I couldn't write! That novel I was working on — I even had a movie contract — I can't remember what I did with the manuscript. I might even have burned it. I was out of my head with grief and behaving like a crazy man."

"If you couldn't work, what were you doing in Louisiana?" I demanded. "You wrote me that you were coming here on a business trip."

"That's true," Dad said. "*Travel and Leisure* wanted a

8

story on the Mardi Gras. That assignment was my agent's doing, not mine. He was hoping that the pressure of a deadline might get me working again. I let him talk me into it. I thought he might be right. If I could get away from that empty house — from the memories — then maybe . . ."

He let the sentence trail off.

"That's where you met Lisette? At Mardi Gras?"

Dad nodded. "It was at a ball at the Convention Center. I'll never forget how she looked the first time I saw her. She was dressed all in white, in an old-fashioned gown with a hoopskirt. There was lace at her throat, and she wore camellias in her hair. I caught sight of her across the dance floor, and I just stood there, staring like a schoolboy. She had to be the most beautiful woman I'd ever seen in my life."

I could not let that statement pass unchallenged.

"More beautiful than Mother?"

"That's not fair," Dad said shortly.

"But, you *said* it!"

"Your mother was dear and lovely. She had an inner beauty. It made me happy just to look at her sweet face."

"But she wasn't movie-star-glamorous, like your Lisette is!"

"No, she wasn't." The silence that followed seemed to last forever. Then, Dad said quietly, "Don't do this to me, Nore. Don't try to ruin it. Can't you just be happy that I've finally come alive again? Your mother would have been." He paused. "Well, *wouldn't* she? Be honest."

As much as I hated to, I had to answer, "Yes."

"This is another chapter of life for me," Dad continued. "It's no disloyalty to your mother or to our good marriage. It's the same for Lisette, a second chance at happiness. She's

9

a wonderful woman and hasn't had it easy. A widow, raising two kids on next to no money — that's rough."

"What are her children like?" I asked, curious despite myself. "You hardly mentioned them in your letter."

"Gabe, the boy, is about your age. He's a bright, attractive kid. I think you'll like him. Josie's at that awkward stage, just going into her teens. She's going to be a beauty one day, you can tell, but it'll take a few years."

"What do they call you?"

If he had told me, "Dad," I think I would have burst into tears, but, to my relief, he didn't.

"They call me 'Chuck,' just like everybody else does. And they're keeping their own last name, 'Bergé.' Of course, you'll call Lisette by her given name — no 'Mom'-type thing. She won't be trying to take your mother's place, Nore. I don't expect you to be her daughter, but I do hope you'll be her friend. Will you try?"

He was backing me to the wall. I had no choice.

I drew in a long breath and let it out slowly.

"I'll try," I said reluctantly. "I can't promise anything more than that, but I'll try."

With that exchange behind us, there seemed suddenly to be nothing left to talk about. We continued to drive for another half hour or so, making sporadic attempts at casual conversation. During that time, the terrain that slid past the car windows underwent a number of changes. The woodlands gave away to fields and then to marshland. Our road adhered to the bank of a narrow, brown river, which Dad said was a tributary of the Mississippi. Occasionally, he would draw my attention to some feature of the scenery — "That's a heron. See, out in the water, that big white bird?" or "Look over there on that tree; that's a wild orchid," or

10

"That may look like bamboo, but it's actually sugarcane."

Ahead of us, the sun was rapidly sliding lower in the sky. I leaned my head back against the seat and blinked into the glare, trying to get my thoughts in order, but finding that almost impossible. The effects of the heat and humidity, piled on top of a sleepless night of nervous anticipation, were catching up with me.

I was just beginning to doze a little, when my father said, "Here we are. This is the entrance to Shadow Grove."

"It is?" My eyes snapped open, and I glanced in bewilderment from one side of the road to the other. "But, we're out in the middle of nowhere!"

To our left there was nothing to be seen but the marshes and the river behind them. On our right, the road was bordered by a wrought-iron fence, half concealed by an overgrowth of high, flowering bushes. No house was in evidence, although some fifty yards ahead of us the line of the fence was broken by an open gate.

"The old plantation homes were always in the rural areas," Dad said. "Many, like Shadow Grove, date back to before the Civil War. This estate was originally owned by the prosperous DuBois family, and they presented it to their daughter as a wedding gift when she married a man named Bergé back in the eighteen seventies. That was an era when cotton and sugarcane were the life blood of Louisiana. Industry in the cities came later."

We pulled through the gate into the drive beyond it. There, I found myself confronted by one of the most spectacular sights I had ever seen. On either side of the driveway, there stood a line of huge oak trees, their giant branches intertwining to form a massive canopy of vibrant green. Through the spaces between the leaves, the late afternoon sunlight fell in golden splashes, painting intricate patterns on the driveway below. At the far end of this incredible corridor, there stood what appeared to be a mansion, but, framed as it was by the immense trees, it was impossible to determine its true size. Although its proportions implied the magnitude of a great cathedral, it was so dwarfed by the towering oaks that it gave the illusion of being no larger than a child's miniature model.

As we moved slowly up the driveway, it began to assume its proper place as the focal point of the scene before us. The closer we drew, the more impressive the structure became. It stood three stories high, if you chose to count the ground-floor level as a story. The wide-porched main floor stood well above this and was supported by brick pillars and edged on both sides by a parade of graceful white columns. A balcony extended the length of the highest level, and above that there rose a steeply pitched roof.

"It's like something out of *Gone With the Wind!*" I exclaimed in amazement.

"Yes, it is," Dad agreed. "Or, rather, it used to be. You can't tell from here, but the years and the weather have taken their toll. We're in the process now of getting the place reroofed, and I'm afraid we may have to completely rebuild the porches and balconies."

We continued on up the leaf-shaded driveway, and Dad brought the car to a stop in front of the house. On the porch, a woman stood waiting.

Our eyes met and held, while Lisette and I took stock of each other.

My father's description had not done this woman justice. She was more than beautiful. Small and slightly built, she had the fragile perfection of a princess from a fairy tale. Her heavily lashed, dark eyes accentuated the delicately chiseled features of her face. Glossy, black hair, swept high and held in place by golden combs, gave her a look of elegance that belied her small stature. Most startling of all was her complexion. The creamy skin was totally free of lines or blemishes and had a look of such taut and youthful freshness that it did not seem possible that it could belong to a woman with teenage children.

This is Lisette, I thought incredulously. *This is my father's wife.*

"Be her friend," Dad had begged me. "Will you try?"

Now, as I sat, staring up at my stepmother, I suddenly realized that this choice was not going to be mine to make. Despite the childlike loveliness of her face and figure, the tiny woman on the porch above me radiated strength. It would be Lisette, not I, who would be making the decisions here at Shadow Grove.

And, as for friendship —

I stared into those luminous eyes, and a chill shot through me. What I saw there was not the promise of friendship, but of something strange and sinister.

The shocking word that flashed through my mind was "death."

CHAPTER

2

Which, of course, was ridiculous. In the next instant, whatever small thing it was that had triggered such a reaction on my part — a trick of the light, perhaps, or my own overactive imagination — had righted itself, and the beautiful eyes held nothing but warmth and welcome.

Lisette, smiling and gracious, came hurrying down the steps to greet me. She was wearing a peach-colored dress with a full, swirling skirt, and her slim, white arms were as creamy and smooth as her face.

"Eleanor!" she exclaimed in a voice that had the same rich, musical quality as those I had overheard while waiting for Dad to bring the car from the airport parking lot. "Eleanor, dear, welcome to Shadow Grove! I can't tell you how happy we are to have you with us!"

"Thank you," I said a bit stiffly. "It's nice to be here. It was my mother, though, who was Eleanor. I go by Nore."

"Of course," Lisette said apologetically. "That shows how

excited I am; I'm not even thinking straight! Your father has talked so much about both you and your wonderful mother that her name comes popping out as naturally as yours does."

By this time, Dad had gotten out of the car and was coming around to open the door on my side. This was something I had never known him to do before.

Lisette, however, seemed to take the courtesy for granted, and kept chatting, lightly and easily, as Dad took my hand and pulled me to my feet.

"Your father says you've never spent time in the South before. I hope you'll learn to love it here as much as we do. There's some strange magic about this bayou country. Those of us who were born here may move other places, but we always seem to come back again."

As Dad unloaded the suitcases, Lisette linked her arm through mine and drew me up the porch steps and through the open doorway into the entrance hall. Beyond this was the living room, or — as I would learn to call it — the "parlor," a long, narrow room with floor-to-ceiling windows that opened out upon a courtyard. The room's walls were plastered white, and these, along with the extremely high ceiling and the direct exposure to the out-of-doors, gave it a feeling of airy spaciousness. The furniture was composed entirely of antiques — graceful high-backed chairs and inlaid tables, a glass case containing an assortment of old fashioned firearms, and ornate, gold-rimmed mirrors. On one wall, over an upright piano, there hung an oil painting of a bearded man in an old-fashioned frock coat, and at the far end of the room, flanked by dark wood end tables, there stood a sofa upholstered in rose-colored velvet.

A young man was seated there, reading. As Lisette and I

came into the room, he laid his book aside and sprang hastily to his feet.

"This is my son, Gabriel," said Lisette. "Gabe, dear, this is Chuck's daughter, Nore."

"Hi, Nore! It's nice to meet you." Gabe flashed me a friendly smile and extended his hand. Small-boned and compactly built, he stood only an inch or so taller than I. This was more than compensated for, however, by a face that could have graced an album cover. The high, fine cheekbones, sensuous mouth, and dark brown eyes made any rock star I'd ever seen look like leftover nothing.

"It's nice to meet you, too," I said, trying to sound casual as I took the proffered hand.

"Lis," Dad said from the doorway, "where should I take these bags? Have you decided yet which room you want to give Nore?"

"I thought she might like the rose room," said Lisette. "That's a corner room, Nore, so you'll get a nice flow of air. These lovely old relics of houses weren't designed for modern air conditioning, but they were built high enough from the ground so they do catch the breezes."

My initial reaction to Shadow Grove as a replica of Scarlet O'Hara's Tara was renewed and reinforced as Dad, Lisette and I mounted the winding stairway to the upper level of the house. The staircase itself was built of Louisiana cypress, my father informed me, sounding as proud of the fact as if he had hewn the trees himself, and the banister was of a rich, dark mahogany of such fine grain that it slid beneath the palm of my hand like satin. The long row of bedrooms was located on a central hallway, but each room had as well a large, louvered door that opened onto the balcony. The rose room — which, evidently, drew its name from the pattern of tiny rosebuds on the wallpaper — had two such doors, one to the north, facing out upon the driveway, and one to the east, where an array of colorful flower beds bordered a brick path that led down to what appeared to be a lily pond.

"Leave the jalousies open, and you'll be surprised at how cool you'll stay at night," Lisette told me. "You'd better pull the screens, though, or you'll be eaten alive by mosquitoes. Those pink towels on the bureau are yours. You and my daughter, Josie, who has the bedroom next to this one, will be sharing the bath across the hall. Your father and I have the master bedroom at the center of the house, and Gabe's room is on the far west end."

"Where would you like me to set these suitcases?" my father asked me.

"It doesn't matter," I said. "Just anywhere."

"I imagine you'd like to get freshened up and rest before dinner," said Lisette. "We won't be eating until seven or so, so you'll have time to take a nap or get unpacked or do anything else you'd like. I've put some empty hangers in the closet for you. If there's anything else you need, just let me know."

"Thank you," I said. "It seems as though you've thought of everything."

"If I haven't, be sure and tell me," Lisette said warmly. "I want you to be happy here, Nore. Shadow Grove is *your* home now, just as it's ours. I hope that you'll learn to love it as dearly as we do."

Impulsively, she leaned over and kissed me on the cheek. The brush of her lips was as soft as the wings of a butterfly.

For one brief moment, I breathed in the scent of gardenias.

Then Lisette drew back, smiling, and reached for my father's hand.

"Nore must be tried after her long trip, Chuck. Let's give her a little time to herself."

"That's a good idea." Dad smiled too. I could tell that he was pleased that our meeting had gone so smoothly. "You come on down when you're ready, baby. By then, maybe, Josie will be back from wherever it is she's wandered off to, and you'll get to meet the third member of your new family."

They left the room, still holding hands, and I stood, listening to the receding sound of their footsteps as they echoed down the hall. Suddenly, they stopped. There was the sound of a door being opened and then softly closed. Then, there was silence.

I went over to the doorway and stared out into the empty hall. Instead of going downstairs, Dad and Lisette had evidently entered their bedroom.

Their bedroom. The thought of my father's sharing a room with someone other than my mother was so foreign to me that it was almost inconceivable. What were they doing now? I wondered. Kissing? Whispering love words? Were they standing on the far side of that closed door, locked in each other's arms?

It was a question, I knew, that I had no business pondering. I must learn to accept the fact that my father was now remarried. As he, himself, had pointed out to me, another chapter of his life was beginning, and he was obviously head-over-heels in love with his beautiful new wife.

Shoving the vision of the embracing couple out of my mind, I pushed my own door closed and turned my attention to the suitcases that Dad had set on the floor at the end of the four-poster bed. For the next quarter-hour or so, I kept myself busy hanging dresses in the closet and loading piles of shorts, T-shirts and underwear into drawers of the bureau. I carried my toothbrush and other toiletries across the hall to the bathroom, where I found the medicine cabinet jammed to overflowing with more bottles and jars of blusher, foundation and eye shadow than a fashion model could have put to use in a lifetime. Josie must be a precocious thirteen-year-old, I thought with amusement, as I shuffled things about to try to create a space in which to set my own lone tube of mascara.

Returning to the rose room, I unpacked my hairdryer and curling iron, a cassette player with an assortment of tapes, and my camera. Finally, when everything else had been taken care of, I removed from the side pocket of the second suitcase a small, framed photograph of my mother.

I had taken the snapshot myself, and it showed Mother, dressed in a plaid shirt and blue jeans, standing in the front yard of our home in Guilderland. We had just returned from a bike ride, and her hair was a mass of windblown curls. She was facing the camera, laughing, and in the background, propped against the house, there stood a bicycle. It was the same red ten-speed that she was to be riding three days later when a prominent local businessman, rushing back to his office after a three-martini lunch, ran a stop sign.

Cupping the photograph in my hands, I sat down on the edge of the bed to study the beloved face. No, my mother had not been a glamour queen by anybody's standards, and, most certainly, she could not have competed in looks with Lisette. Mother had been, for one thing, a good twelve years older. My parents had been in their mid-thirties when I was born, and this picture showed a woman with laugh lines at the corners of her eyes and worry lines on her forehead and a few extra pounds on her hips and around her waist. She was simply *herself* — "Eleanor Robbins, housewife and mother" — after years of being "Eleanor Robbins, computer programmer." Although she had been good at her job, she had never been a career woman. The day that Dad's eighth novel, *Life in the Fast Lane,* had sold to Hollywood, Mother had happily retired from the work force to become a full-time homemaker.

"You're going to be bored stiff," her career-minded friends had warned her. "What on earth will you find to do with yourself all day?"

"All the things I've never had time to do," Mother had told them. "I've got enough projects lined up to keep me busy for the rest of my life."

The word "boredom" didn't exist for Mother. How excited she had been at the thought of all the adventures that lay in store for her! How unfair it was that "the rest of her life," which she had been so eagerly looking forward to, had consisted of only three short years!

Blinking against the familiar sting of unshed tears, I leaned back upon the pillows and closed my eyes. The face in the photograph continued to smile at me from the inside of my closed eyelids.

Unfair! my mind screamed in silent protest. *Unfair!*

After so many years of struggle to make ends meet, my parents had finally seen their dream become reality. *Life in the Fast Lane* had become the pilot of a prime-time television series, and, overnight, Dad's income had leapt well into the six-figure bracket. The saying "Success breeds success" had proved to be true in my father's case. Once the name "Charles Robbins" had become recognized, Dad's earlier novels had suddenly been rediscovered. They were hailed as "lively reads" by those very reviewers who had previously ignored them, and paperback houses had fought to outbid each other for publication rights.

It was the classic happy ending to the "rags to riches" story, except that Mother, who should have been enjoying it with us, was gone. It would be Lisette, not Eleanor Robbins, who would be sharing the second half of my father's life with him, and although he had not revealed the fact in his letter, I was beginning to suspect that this life would be spent at Shadow Grove.

"I'd like for us all to spend the summer together," Dad had written. "It will give us a chance to become a united family. Lisette owns a house here that has been sitting unoccupied. I want to devote this summer to putting it back into shape again."

At the time I read it, I had interpreted that statement to mean that Dad was planning to get the house fixed up for sale. Now, however, I had to believe otherwise. Lisette had been so adamant about the fact that Shadow Grove was home to her that I couldn't imagine her consenting to move to Guilderland.

Why, then, I wondered, had she and her children ever left here? As attached as they were to Shadow Grove, why had they moved away? Wouldn't it have been more natural for Lisette, as a single parent, to have wanted to raise her son and daughter in this home that they all seemed to love so dearly?

After the pressures of the day, the clammy heat was affecting me like a sedative. One moment I was lucid and thinking rationally, and the next I had slipped across the line into dreaming. Cloud wisps blew through my groggy mind like whirling shreds of cotton, and a canopy of oak leaves closed in above me.

A hand touched my cheek, and when, in the dream, my eyes flew open, it was to find my mother standing by my bedside.

I was not surprised. I had such dreams quite often.

"Mother," I said, "what are you doing here? You're supposed to be *dead!*"

"Not to you," the familiar voice said matter-of-factly. "I'm not dead to *you,* Nore. Now listen, because I have something important to tell you. I want you to repack your things and leave Shadow Grove immediately."

"Leave Shadow Grove?" I exclaimed. "But, I've only just got here! Dad wants me to spend the summer. In September, I'll be going back to school in New England."

"By September, it will be too late," my mother told me. "You and your father are both in terrible danger. You must talk to Dad, you must tell him — *Nore, are you listening?*"

But, I wasn't any longer. Caught in the tides of sleep, I was drifting away from her, and the shreds of blowing cotton were becoming a snowstorm. The branches of the oak trees were dipping lower and lower, and their leaves were sending shadows flickering across the fading image of Mother's face.

It did not occur to me then to take this dream-warning seriously. It was not as though this were the first time I'd seen my mother when I was sleeping. Such grief visions spattered my nights with regularity.

I'm a reasonable person; I don't believe in ghosts.

What I have learned to believe in is something far more frightening.

CHAPTER

--•≺ 3 ≻•--

WHEN I awoke, the air had grown somewhat cooler and the room was soft with the gentle hues of twilight. The sun had slid below the treeline, and the light that slipped in through the open louvers of the two French doors was muted and diffused.

I knew instinctively that it was almost seven, the time Lisette had set for dinner. I don't have many talents, but one that I do possess is an acute awareness of time. I can somehow sense what time it is, almost to the minute, and I can wake myself up at a predetermined hour without setting an alarm clock.

My muscles were so stiff that it was evident I'd slept without moving. The photograph of my mother was still clutched in my hands.

You and your father are in terrible danger!

"It was a dream, just another dream," I reassured myself.

The woman in the picture seemed to be smiling in agreement.

"How silly the two of us are!" she might have been saying. "The next time I come into your dreams, I'll say something more sensible."

Getting up from the bed, I placed the framed photograph carefully on the bureau top and went across to the bathroom to get washed up for dinner. The face that gazed back at me from the mirror over the sink was flushed and puffy-eyed from an overdose of sleep. I doused it with cold water, dabbed some lipstick on my mouth, and dragged a comb through my tangle of pillow-matted hair. Then, on impulse, I got my mascara out of the medicine cabinet and applied it to both my upper and lower lashes. I told myself that I wanted to look nice so that Dad would be proud of me, but I have to admit I had another reason as well. If his mother was an example of what women in Louisiana looked like, Gabe Bergé would be used to some pretty exotic girls.

Back in my bedroom, I peeled off my damp blouse and travel-rumpled cords and dropped them into one of my newly emptied suitcases. Then, I went over to the closet and got out the frilliest piece of clothing I possessed, a sleeveless, yellow sundress with a full, ruffled skirt. I'm the type of person who runs to pants and pullovers, and I'd never felt comfortable about that impulsive purchase. Now, though, cinching in the belt and swaying my hips a little to cause the soft material to swirl out away from my legs, I felt pleased with my mental picture of how I must look. If femininity was the byword for ladies at Shadow Grove, I'd show the Bergés I could hold my own with the best of them.

Downstairs, I found Dad, Lisette and Gabe seated in the parlor, sipping amber liquid from delicate, long-stemmed glasses.

Dad looked up with a smile when he saw me in the doorway.

"What did I tell you, Lis?" he said with satisfaction. "Here she is on the dot of seven, and she's not even wearing a watch."

"Not a moment late nor a moment early. That's really incredible!" Lisette smiled also. "Your father's been telling us about this gift of yours, Nore. I thought one of us had better go up and wake you, but he told me that you have your own built-in alarm clock."

"It's too bad that Josie doesn't have one," Gabe commented dryly. "Then maybe she'd turn up for things when she's supposed to."

"You're right about that. It would certainly make life easier." Lisette continued to smile with her lips, but not with her eyes. "Josie's not home yet, Nore, so dinner will be later than I intended. While we're waiting, can I offer you a glass of sherry?"

"No, thank you," I said, surprised at the invitation. Our family had never been into the cocktail-hour bit.

"A Coke, then?" Lisette was asking, when there came the sound of the front door being thrown open and slammed shut again.

"She's here," said Gabe. "You can relax now, Maman. The wanderer's returned."

"Josie?" There was a strident edge to Lisette's voice. "Josie, come in here this instant! Do you have any idea how late it is?"

"Sorry, Maman. I lost track of time."

The girl who appeared in the doorway was small and dark, with Lisette's high cheekbones and luminous brown eyes. One day, perhaps, her beauty would match her mother's, but at this point nothing about her had come into proportion. Her nose was too long, her mouth too wide, her chest still flat and bony, and she had the overall gawky look of a knobby-kneed colt.

Her appearance brought back painful memories of my own transition from childhood to adolescence. I breathed a sigh of relief that this stage of life now lay behind me.

"You have a watch, Jo," said Lisette. "Why aren't you wearing it?"

"I forgot to put it on after my shower last night." The girl turned her attention to me. "You're Chuck's daughter, right? You're Nore?"

"Yes, I'm Nore," I said. "It's nice to meet you, Josie."

"Where have you been?" Lisette demanded. "You've been gone for hours!"

"I went for a walk," Josie told her. "Where else would I go, for gosh sakes? It's not like there's anyplace around here where people can have fun. There's no shopping center, no movie, no video arcade. Living out here at Shadow Grove is like being locked into a big moldy old cage."

"That's enough, Jo," Lisette said shortly. "Go get cleaned up. Then come back down and join us in the dining room. If it weren't for the fact that it's Nore's first evening here, you would be skipping dinner."

Josie glared at her mother and muttered some comment under her breath that I did not catch.

Gabe evidently did, however.

"Don't push your luck, kid," he said softly. "You know how Maman feels about your taking off on your own like that. She worries all the time that something will happen to you."

"Well, that's stupid," Josie shot back belligerently. "By now, you both should know that I can take care of myself."

"Jo!" Lisette said warningly.

26

"Okay! Okay! I'm going!" Glowering, Josie turned on her heel and stalked out of the room.

Her departure was followed by an uncomfortable silence. It was Lisette who finally broke it.

"I'm sure that everyone's starving," she said. "There's no good reason why we should wait any long for dinner. Chuck — Nore — I do apologize for my daughter's behavior. I'm afraid she's going through that rebellious stage that you always hear about."

"It hits all kids that age," said Dad, trying to make light of the situation. "When Nore was thirteen, she thought the whole world was against her, especially her parents. Then, just when her mother and I were about ready to ship her off to an orphanage, she came over the hump and turned into a delightful young adult." He rose to his feet and offered his wife his arm. "If the food is ready, *I* certainly am. Let's go get some dinner."

With Dad and Lisette leading the way, we trooped into the dining room, which, like the parlor, had windows that faced out onto the darkening courtyard. An ornate, mahogany china cabinet took up most of the far end of the room, and a crystal chandelier hung suspended from the ceiling over an oval table that was formally set for five.

"Chuck, will you light the candles, please?" Lisette asked my father. "Gabe, dear, come give me a hand, if you will, in bringing things in. No, Nore," — as I started to volunteer my assistance — "tomorrow you can pitch right in with the rest of us, but you deserve one night of being the guest of honor."

So, I took the seat to which she gestured me, and while Dad lit the candles — six tall, white tapers in antique silver holders — Lisette and Gabe trotted back and forth to the kitchen, carrying in bowls of a spicy, tomato-based soup

27

filled with shrimp and crabmeat, and hot French bread, and a tossed green salad.

"I don't understand why you don't hire some live-in help," said my father, as Lisette placed the bowl of salad in the center of the table and then seated herself in the chair on his right. "For a place this size, we ought to have a full-time cook and housekeeper. You know darned well that back in the old times the estate was swarming with servants."

"They used slave labor back then," said Lisette. "Today, household help is terribly expensive. People just don't 'live in' the way they used to."

"We've got the money to spend, hon," my father said gently. "What's the point of my finally having made it big if I can't use the income to make life pleasant for my family?"

"You've spent so much on us already," Lisette protested. "The restoration of Shadow Grove is going to cost a small fortune. Then, on top of that, you've hired a ground maintenance service; you've bought me a washer and dryer; you've had a dishwasher installed; and the other day I heard you promising Josie a swimming pool."

"I want you to have live-in help," Dad repeated stubbornly. "Why are you so set against it, Lis? It can't just be the cost. You know that's not a problem in my present situation."

"I guess maybe I have a thing about privacy," Lisette admitted. "The idea of some stranger living right here with us, snooping on everything we say or do — it just makes me uncomfortable somehow. I did hire that Cajun girl, Celina, to come clean on Wednesdays."

"What's 'Cajun'?" I asked, taking advantage of the sudden lull in the conversation. "I've heard the term, but I don't know exactly what it means."

"The terms 'Cajun' and 'Creole' both refer to the descendants of the first French settlers of Louisiana," my father told me. "The old Creole families consider themselves aristocracy. Their ancestors came here directly from France, while the Cajuns arrived by way of Canada."

"There were cultural differences too," Lisette said crisply. "Many of the early Cajuns intermarried with the natives. The strain has been watered down enough by now so the differences aren't so evident, but several generations ago they were a whole foreign element with their own life-style and customs and weird superstitions."

"What sort of superstitions?" I asked with interest.

"Heavens, *I* don't know." Lisette shrugged her slender shoulders. "It's not a subject that has ever been of much interest to me."

"They might well have been based on voodoo," suggested my father. "Back in the beginning of the nineteenth century, Napoleon's invasion of Cuba drove many of the French-speaking natives to relocate in New Orleans. They brought their pagan religions with them, and from what I've read, voodooism became somewhat of a vogue here even among the whites."

"That's not the case now, thank goodness." Lisette glanced up at the doorway. "Well — Josie — so you've finally decided to join us!"

"I didn't think you were offering me a choice," said Josie. She crossed to the table and slid unceremoniously into the seat next to her brother. Although she was dressed in the same jeans and T-shirt she had been wearing when she came in from her walk, her hair was now combed and she had put on makeup. A lot of makeup.

"Gumbo again?" She wrinkled her nose with a show of

distaste. "You've hardly served anything else since we got back here this time. Can't we ever have pizza the way we did in Chicago?"

"Not if I have anything to say about it," said Lisette. "We're home again now, thank goodness, and I, personally, can't get enough seafood to make up for all of those years we spent away."

"This is great," I said in an effort to compensate for Josie's rudeness. "One of the nice things about going to school in New England is that they serve us fresh seafood. Would you believe that once they even gave us lobster?"

"We lived for a while in Boston," said Gabe. "I liked it there."

Dad turned to Lisette in surprise. "You never told me that!"

"You and I had a whirlwind courtship," Lisette reminded him. "There are lots of things I haven't had a chance to tell you."

"We've lived in loads of big cities," Josie said proudly. "New York, Philadelphia, San Francisco — there have been so many of them that the only way I can tell them apart is if something special happened there. I'll always remember Hartford, for instance, because that's where the Ringling Circus tent caught fire and we almost got trampled to death trying to get out. Then, there was the —"

"That's enough rambling, Jo," Lisette broke in abruptly. "How about talking less and eating more? The rest of us are almost finished with dinner."

"I was just trying to be sociable," Josie said in an injured voice.

"I appreciate that," said Lisette, and I was startled by the edge to her voice. "I would appreciate it more, though, if you would concentrate on eating instead of chattering. After you've finished, I would like you to clear the table and load the dishwasher. No back talk now!" — as Josie's mouth flew open to protest — "This is neither the time nor place for a mother-daughter battle."

Josie seemed about to respond, and then evidently thought better of it. Throwing her mother a black look, she lapsed into sullen silence, which she maintained for the duration of the meal.

When dinner was over, the rest of us moved out into the courtyard and settled into lawn chairs to watch a full moon rise slowly and majestically out of the trees to take its place in the absolute center of the sky. Now that the heat of the day had lessened, the air had a softness to it that was different from anything I had ever felt in the North. The aroma of honeysuckle was all around us, so heavy that I could almost taste the scent of it, and the chanting of cicadas filled the night with so much sound that conversation seemed unnecessary.

Gabe served us all glasses of anisette, which he informed me was a traditional French after-dinner drink. This time I didn't refuse the cordial, and, leaning back in my chair, I sipped the thick, sweet liquid and stared up into the star-studded sky, feeling more at peace than I had in a long, long time.

Perhaps things would be all right after all, I told myself. Lisette had not turned out to be the "wicked stepmother" that I had anticipated. Josie, for all her perversity, was no worse than many other girls her age, craving independence and resenting parental restriction. And Gabe —

My heart gave an odd little jump as I gazed across at Gabe. The moonlight lay in streaks of silver upon his forehead. The rest of his face was lost in shadow, and I could not see his eyes. What was he thinking? I wondered. How did he feel about our sudden entrance into his family? Had it been as hard for him to adjust to the idea as it had been for me? Would he accept me as a sister; and did I *want* him to?

The long, stressful day — the hour's difference in time — the unaccustomed glass of anisette — all were working together to weight my eyelids. A soft breeze blew up from the river to stroke my face, and the song of the crickets was as soothing as a lullaby.

When Dad said, "Nore, are you awake over there?," I tried unsuccessfully to stifle a yawn.

"No," I confessed, "not really. I guess I'd better call it a night before I fall completely asleep in my chair."

So, I said my goodnights and went indoors. As I passed the doorway to the kitchen, I glanced inside, thinking I might stop and exchange a word or two with Josie, but the dishwasher was already running and the room was dark.

I continued on upstairs and down the long hall to the room at the corner. As I was opening my bedroom door, I became aware of the sound of a record player in the adjoining room. Josie had evidently decided against any further socializing and had retired to spend the remainder of the evening in her own company.

Poor kid, I thought, as I put on my pajamas and drew the screens across the doors to the balcony. In my opinion, Lisette had overreacted to the situation in the dining room. Josie had only been trying to sound cosmopolitan when she had bragged about all the places that her family had lived.

Why, I wondered, had they changed residences so often? And why had the places they had lived all been large cities? If Lisette loved the rural aspects of Shadow Grove, it seemed peculiar that she would have chosen to keep moving her family from metropolis to metropolis.

The dinner-table conversation had been general and inconsequential. Still, as I settled myself in bed and reached over to flick off the lamp, I could not help but feel that there had been something that I had missed. Something had been said that had *not* been trivial and meaningless. There had been something — something —

The answer came to me as I was slipping into sleep, and the shock of the realization jolted me awake. Josie had commented that she would always remember Hartford, because she had been living there at the time of the Ringling Brothers Circus fire.

I had heard about that fire from my mother, who had grown up in a small town in rural Connecticut. She had told me about it one day when I was sick in bed with chicken pox.

"I had chicken pox too when I was about your age," she had told me sympathetically. "In my case, though, being sick may have saved my life. My parents were planning to take me to the circus to celebrate my eleventh birthday, but I got sick, so the outing had to be called off. That day a terrible fire broke out in the Ringling circus tent, and a hundred and sixty-eight people died in the blaze."

The date of my mother's eleventh birthday was forty years ago.

CHAPTER

4

GENTLE and sweet-breathed as those early summer evenings may have been, the loveliest time of day at Shadow Grove was morning.

My first day there, I awoke very early because of the time difference between Louisiana and the East Coast. Lying in bed, I could see out through both of the screened French doors, each of which framed a great sheet of empty sky. This sky, as seen through the north door, was pale blue and hazy; to the east, it was aglow with the flames of sunrise. I lay still for a time, watching, mesmerized, as the two special areas went through minute-by-minute alterations. The north sky grew brighter and clearer; the east sky softened to pink, and then, as shade melted into shade in fluid transition, became the same clear blue as its sister next door.

When the two pictures had synchronized, I sat up in bed. From this higher vantage point, I could see the massive green heads of the oak trees through the door to the north. I got out of bed and crossed over to the bureau. My mother's face smiled good morning to me from the snapshot. I pulled open the drawer and got out shorts and a T-shirt and carried them with me across the hall to the bathroom.

As I showered and dressed, I reviewed the previous evening. Now, in the clear light of day, Josie's strange statement affected me less strongly. It had, of course, been untrue. Josie was thirteen years old, and it was obviously impossible for her to have been *anywhere* forty years ago. It must simply have been that she had felt left out of the dinner-table conversation and had wanted to make some remark absurd enough to draw attention to herself. It was evident that the child was extremely lonely. The peace and seclusion at Shadow Grove might be appealing to adults, but for a youngster Josie's age, it meant being cut off from any chance for a normal social life. One lone girl, stuck out in the middle of nowhere, without access to friends or leisuretime activities, might easily become resentful and rebellious. When seen from that point of view, Josie's hostility toward her mother became — though no more pleasant to witness — at least, more understandable.

Well, *I* was here now, I told myself; that might help matters. While I wasn't exactly Josie's contemporary, I came closer to filling that role than anyone else around. Perhaps, I could become her friend as well as her stepsister. If I could, then life might be easier for everyone.

Josie's door was still closed when I came out of the bathroom. I paused at my own bedroom long enough to deposit my pajamas and then continued on down the hall to the stairs. As I descended the staircase, I knew instinctively that none of the others were up and about yet. There was an absolute stillness about the house below me and that made it seem caught and locked in time like the slumbering palace of Sleeping Beauty. I stepped off the bottom stair into the front entrance hall, and the sound of my shoe's striking the wooden floorboards was as startling as gunfire.

Without conscious thought, I found myself walking on tiptoe as I crossed to the entrance to the parlor. Seen without occupants, the room was like a set from a period play, with the antique furniture, the hand-carved mantel, the gold-inlayed scrollwork around the mirrors. The oriental carpet, though worn with the passage of years, glowed softly with muted colors from the past.

At the end of the room, the portrait of the bearded man in the old-fashioned coat looked like something that should have been hanging in a museum. For some reason, however, the face no longer seemed strange to me. It was a moment before I realized that the features of the face, the dark hair and the wiry build very much resembled those of Gabe Bergé.

A great-grandfather, I thought, or perhaps a great-*great*-grandfather. I was not versed enough in the history of men's fashions to be able to place the precise era of the man's clothing, but I guessed it to be from the end of the nineteenth century.

What should I do with myself until the others woke up? I wondered. Back home in Guilderland, I would have gone out to the kitchen and put on the coffee, but to do that in someone else's house seemed pretty presumptuous. It would be better, I decided, to stay clear of Lisette's kitchen until I'd had a chance to find out where she kept things and whether or not she'd appreciate help making breakfast.

Dawn had now given way to full-fledged morning. In the short time that I had been standing at the entrance to the parlor, the light in the room had already changed significantly. When I had come downstairs, it had been dusky with shadows. Now the sun had risen high enough to slant its light in through the southern windows so that it fell in pale strips across the carpet. Through those windows I could see, as I had not been able to the evening before, an assortment of wooden planters filled with orange flowers. Beyond those, there stood a low hedge of flowering bushes, and farther still a line of small, weathered buildings. I decided that since I appeared to have the whole of Shadow Grove to myself right then, I might as well seize the opportunity to do some exploring.

When I let myself out through the front door, the lush beauty of the day burst upon me. There was a richness about it, a thick, golden sweetness, that poured over me like sun-warmed honey. Directly ahead lay the driveway, a sun-spotted corridor, flanked by the incredible oaks. At its far end, the wrought-iron gate stood open to the road. When I glanced to either side of me, greenery and flowers were everywhere, in some cases so dense that they could have passed for a tropical jungle. Spanish moss and honeysuckle hung draped from branches, and magnolia trees were heavy with bursting blossoms. Tiny hummingbirds, their wings whirling like miniature helicopters, hung suspended beside the thick bushes of crepe myrtle that rose to cushion the warped edges of the porch.

I descended the porch steps and walked slowly along the front of the house, almost overpowered by the scent of so many intermingled perfumes. As I rounded the northeast corner, I came upon the brick path that I had viewed from my bedroom window the afternoon before. It was bordered by beds of iris, and beyond those there rose a tangle of rosebushes sporting blooms that ranged from the palest pink to a crimson so deep that it was almost purple.

Distracted from my original purpose, I paused a moment, trying to decide whether to continue on around to the back of the house or to take the path. I decided on the latter, and several moments later was standing on the bank of a small, circular pond, the surface of which was so solidly covered with lily pads that the water beneath them was totally invisible. This green carpet was broken at intervals by waxen blossoms, floating lazily with petals spread to the sky.

"Nore! Hey — Nore!"

Turning in surprise, I saw Gabe jogging toward me across the wide stretch of lawn that lay between the rose garden and the house. He was dressed in shorts and a tank top and running shoes, and his glossy hair reflected the morning sunlight like polished ebony.

"Hi!" he said as drew abreast of me. "What are you doing up so early? Isn't this supposed to be your vacation time?"

"I'm geared to a different time zone," I reminded him. "What's *your* excuse? Isn't this *your* school vacation too?"

"I like to do my running before the heat comes up," Gabe told me. "That's about all the exercise I get these days, and I want to do it right. Back in Chicago, our apartment was right near a fitness center, and I got to work out on all the machines whenever I wanted to."

"Your mother was saying last night that you might get a swimming pool," I said.

"Yeah, Josie's pushing for one," Gabe said wryly. "But, then, Josie pushes for everything. If she had her way, your dad would put in a movie theater, a skating rink and her own private video arcade."

"She must get bored in the summer," I said sympathetically. "Having a pool to swim in could make a big difference."

"She can swim in the river now, or here in the lily pond." Gabe threw me a devilish grin. "Do you want an adventure? Why don't we go back to the house and put on our suits?"

"Not me!" I said vehemently, not certain whether or not he was joking. "I don't know how to swim, and if I *did*, I wouldn't swim in *this!*"

"I was just kidding!" Gabe said. "This pond's two feet deep; *nobody* could swim in it. My kid brother and I used to wade here, though, when we were little. We'd get ourselves coated with mud and then go running back into the house. Maman would scream her head off for fear we'd jump on the furniture."

"Your brother!" I exclaimed. "You and Josie have a *brother?*"

"We did once," said Gabe, the laughter fading from his voice. "Louis died a long time back. He was thrown by a horse. It was a stallion — really wild — he should never have been riding it. Lou was like that, a sort of a daredevil. He did crazy things."

"That's awful," I said.

"It was awful, all right. Maman about went crazy. She just couldn't face the fact that one of her children was dead."

"I know," I said, nodding. "I feel that same way about my mother. I still can't believe that she's gone. I see her in dreams, and it's almost as though she were right there with me."

"You must miss her a lot," Gabe said softly.

"Yes," I said. "But, you know what that's like. You must feel that way about your dad and brother."

"It's not quite the same," Gabe said. "I do miss Louis,

but, like I said, he was killed a long time ago, so I've had time to get used to it. What I miss most now is the whole idea of having a brother. If Lou were here today, he'd be somebody I could talk to. He'd understand my problems, because they'd be the same as his."

"What about your father?" I asked. "What happened to *him?*"

"He got sick," Gabe said shortly.

"Sick, how? With what sort of illness?"

"I don't know. He was old; it could have been a lot of things. One night he went to sleep, and he just stopped breathing. A servant found him when she went in to take him breakfast. That wasn't the shock to us that Lou's death was. Papa'd had a full life."

"He couldn't have been all *that* old," I said. "Your mother's still so young."

"Papa was a lot older. It was a May-December marriage." Gabe drew a deep breath. "Hey, enough of this depressing stuff. Let's talk about something pleasant. What was it that brought you out here this morning so early?"

"I was curious about the old buildings out beyond the courtyard," I told him. "I thought I'd go see what they were, and then, when I saw the path through the rose garden, I decided to walk down here and see what the pond was like."

"Those buildings once served as quarters for slaves," said Gabe. "Come on around back, and I'll show them to you. They're a piece of American history that you really shouldn't miss."

So we walked together to the south side of the house, where the past lay spread before us in depressing dishevelment. The buildings that I had seen through the parlor windows proved to be brick and wood shacks that were so dilapidated that it was hard to imagine anyone's ever having lived in them. Gaping doorways and paneless windows stared blindly out upon fields of underbrush that had once supplied produce enough to feed a whole plantation. Only the cottage nearest to the house, which Gabe informed me was now used as a storage shed, appeared to be in good repair. The windows of that had been bricked over, and its sturdy door was secured with a padlock.

Behind the shacks, there stood the shell of what once must have been a huge and impressive stable.

"Maman got rid of the horses after Louis died," Gabe told me.

"What's that over there?" I asked him, gesturing off to the right, where a wrought-iron fence enclosed what appeared to be a tiny graveyard. It was so overgrown that the rounded tops of two tombstones could barely be seen beneath the tangle of vines and grasses.

"That's the Bergé cemetery," Gabe informed me. "All the old plantations had family burial plots."

"It looks old, all right," I commented. "And it surely could use weeding. Didn't your mother say that Dad had hired a maintenance service?"

"They haven't had time to work on the cemetery yet," said Gabe. "There's been too much else for them to do around the estate. You should have seen this place when we first moved back here. It was a full-fledged jungle."

As we started back toward the house, he reached over and took my hand. "So, what's your reaction? Does Shadow Grove meet your expectations?"

"I'm not sure exactly what it was that I did expect," I told him.

"There are other houses like this one all up and down the

41

river," Gabe said. "They cost so much to keep up that only a handful are still private residences. Most are owned by the state and are used as tourist attractions."

When we entered the house, we found the rest of the family at the breakfast table. The rich aroma of freshly brewed coffee filled the kitchen, and a pitcher of orange juice sat out on the counter.

"Well, hi!" Dad said in surprise. "I didn't expect the two of you to appear together like this. I thought Nore was still upstairs sleeping and Gabe was out running."

"I was," Gabe said, dropping my hand like a hot potato. "Hi, Chuck. Good morning, Maman. Josie, that's one huge bowl of Sugar Pops. Don't you think it would have been nice to have saved some for the rest of us?"

Josie shrugged her shoulders. Her eyes flicked up at her brother. Then she shifted her gaze to her mother, as though curious to see her reaction to the fact that Gabe and I had been holding hands.

I, too, glanced across at Lisette. Her eyes had narrowed strangely, and her full, soft lips were pressed so tightly together that they were compacted into a pencil-thin line.

"So, what have you two early birds been doing?" she asked with a show of casualness. "Don't tell me that Nore's into running too! Are we really to have two exercise buffs at Shadow Grove?"

"I went out by myself like I always do," Gabe said defensively. He hooked his thumbs nervously under the band of his running shorts. "Nore just happened to be up early, and we ran into each other by accident. I took her around in back to have a look at the slave quarters."

"Those buildings are interesting, aren't they? They make the past seem so terribly recent." Although she was ad-

42

dressing herself to me, Lisette's eyes were on Gabe. There seemed to be some sort of unspoken dialogue going on between them, like a secret second level of communication. "The present, as we know it, is of such small importance in the total scheme of things. Its only real purpose is to serve as a bridge between yesterday and tomorrow."

Josie continued to chew methodically on a mouthful of cereal, but she, too, seemed in some way a part of this odd conversation.

Watching the silent interplay between mother and children, I experienced once again the feeling that I was missing out on something. It was as though these three family members had known each other so long and so intimately that they no longer found it necessary to communicate with words.

CHAPTER

⸫⸱⸱❦ 5 ❧⸱⸱⸫

THEN the moment was over. Everything popped back to normal.

What kind of suspicious weirdo are you, Nore? I chided myself.

From the moment I had first arrived at Shadow Grove the atmosphere had kept swinging back and forth between normalcy and strangeness so sporadically that I was never quite sure which end of the seesaw was up. It was as if I kept catching glimpses of something at the edge of my peripheral vision, but it wouldn't hold still long enough for me to get it into focus. One moment, I would be viewing my stepmother as threatening, and ten seconds later she would be chatting along in such a warmhearted manner that I would feel ridiculous for ever having entertained such a thought.

This was one of those times. I felt like a total idiot.

Lisette poured juice into glasses for Gabe and me. I thanked her for mine and sat down in the vacant seat across from my father. Gabe got out two more bowls from the cabinet to the left of the sink, and he and I poured ourselves Rice Crispies (Josie had, indeed, consumed all the Sugar Pops), and if a camera crew had happened to walk in on us right at that particular moment, we could have served as models for a "get-your-family-off-to-a-happy-start-at-breakfasttime" TV commercial.

While we ate, we discussed our plans for the upcoming day.

My father announced that he would be spending it writing.

"I'm back on the job again, Nore," he said with satisfaction. "The dry spell is over. The juices are flowing again, thank God."

"That's terrific!" I exclaimed. "Are you working on another novel?"

"Yes," said Dad, "and it's different from anything I've ever tackled. It's laid here in the South right after the Civil War. I've never tried my hand before at anything historical. I guess the ghosts at Shadow Grove have started to get to my brain."

"In that case, I won't even ask if you want to drive into Merveille with me," said Lisette. "I have to go in to buy groceries and do some errands. I'd enjoy your company, but I don't want it on my conscience that I was the one responsible for stopping the flow of words that could have immortalized Shadow Grove."

"While you're in town, please try to remember to stop by the phone company," said Dad. "I hate this business of being cut off from the world without a telephone."

"Can I go with you?" Josie asked eagerly. "We're all out of munchies, and you never buy anything good unless I'm there."

"Why don't all four of us go?" Gabe suggested. "While

45

you two are doing the grocery shopping, I can show Nore around the metropolis of Merveille."

"That's a laugh!" Josie snorted contemptuously. " 'The metropolis of Merveille'! Still, almost anything's more exciting than hanging around Shadow Grove."

Lisette turned to me with a smile. "I'd love to have you ride in with me, Nore, but don't expect too much of Merveille. As Josie implies, it's not exactly a second New Orleans. You can come too, Jo, but I'd rather that Gabe stayed here. The work on the roof is supposed to be completed today, and someone should be here in case the men finish early."

"Chuck will be here," said Gabe.

"Chuck is going to be working on his book."

"That's no problem," Dad said. "I won't be exactly entombed, you know. I can take an occasional break to check on the workmen."

"I'd like for Gabe to stay," Lisette said again decidedly. "Please, don't argue, son," she added, as Gabe opened his mouth to protest the proclamation. "Chuck has work to do, and I don't want him to be interrupted. Girls, let's try to get started as soon as we're through with breakfast. If possible, I'd like to get back before the work on the roof is finished, so I can check and see that the workmen have cleaned up their litter."

When breakfast was over, I excused myself and hurried up to my bedroom to change into a blouse and skirt in lieu of my shorts. By the time I came back downstairs, Lisette and Josie had already gone out to the car. I was just headed out the front door to join them, when my father called after me, "Nore, will you do me a favor? While Lis is doing errands, could you stop by the library and pick up some reference books?"

"Sure," I said, pausing in the doorway. "What books do you want?"

"I'm not certain myself," Dad said. "I need background material on this part of the country. Just browse the shelves and bring back anything that you think looks interesting."

"Won't I need a card?" I asked him.

"I applied for one a couple of weeks ago," Dad said. "Check with the librarian. She should have it ready for me by this time."

The car that awaited me in the driveway was a dark blue two-door Chevrolet Monte Carlo. Lisette was seated behind the wheel, and Josie was impatiently bouncing up and down in the backseat.

"I'm sorry to have kept you waiting," I said apologetically as I climbed into the passenger's seat next to my stepmother. "Dad stopped me to ask if I'd pick up some books at the library."

"That's easy enough," said Lisette. "The library's right around the corner from the telephone company. You can be picking out the books while I'm making arrangements to get a phone installed."

As we pulled out onto the road through the open gateway, we drove past a green truck which was obviously preparing to turn into the driveway. From the position in which I was seated, I wasn't able to take in much more than the fact that the vehicle had "Parlange Roofing Company" lettered on its side.

Josie, however, let loose with a piercing wolf whistle.

"Hey, Nore!" she exclaimed. "Did you get a load of that guy who was driving? Isn't he a *hunk?*"

"I really couldn't see him too well," I responded, trying to sound regretful. "I'm sitting on the wrong side of the car."

"Well, you really missed something! Wow-*ee!*" Josie

whistled again, hitting a strident note that came close to shattering my eardrums.

With difficulty, I kept from wincing.

Lisette made no such effort.

"Jo," she said, "have you any idea how crude you sound?"

"I don't see what's so crude about noticing a good-looking guy," said Josie peevishly. "He's nice, too. His name is Dave, and I talk to him every day during his lunch break. Did you see the size of his shoulders? They have to be three feet wide!"

"That's enough, Jo," her mother said curtly. "Let's leave that subject, please. Nore, I'll bet you've never seen orchids growing wild before, have you? There are some lovely ones over there in the fork of that oak tree."

"Dad pointed some out to me yesterday," I told her. "It's hard to believe that they grow right out by the roadside here, as common as daisies are back home in New York state."

And so, while Josie sat, sulking, in the seat behind us, Lisette and I continued to make chitchat throughout the remainder of the forty-mile drive into Merveille, a town that turned out to be not much different from what I had been led to expect. As Lisette had warned me, it was certainly no "second New Orleans," but there were enough stores and office buildings to take care of most people's everyday needs.

As we drove through the streets, I saw several grocery stores that I recognized as part of national chains, as well as a Walgreen's, the golden arches of McDonald's, and a J. C. Penney department store like the one in which Mother had bought our towels and bed linens back in Guilderland. There appeared to be only one movie theater, but the marquee advertised a picture that I had seen only recently in Boston, so I gathered that Merveille wasn't all that terribly behind the times.

" 'The Teen Dance Machine'!" Josie squealed in excitement, bouncing out of her surliness. "Look over there on the corner! Do you see that sign? They've turned the old sandwich restaurant into a disco!"

"I'm going to park in the Safeway parking lot," Lisette told us. "That's a good central spot, considering the things we have to do here. The telephone company is just around the corner, and that building across the street is the public library. Why don't we split forces and do our various errands, and then we can meet back at the market to shop for groceries?"

"I want to case-out the disco!" announced Josie.

"At ten in the morning? It'll be locked up and empty." Lisette regarded her daughter with amusement. "Go along to the library with Nore, Jo. You can use Chuck's new card to check out some books for yourself."

"I'm sick of books," Josie grumbled. "It seems like all I've done for a hundred years is read."

Despite her complaints, however, when we reached the library, she did head straight for the section marked "Recent Acquisitions" and began to thumb through the new selection of romance novels.

On checking through the card catalogue, I was pleased to find that the stacks contained a large selection of books on Louisiana history. Settling myself at a table to sort through the volumes, I was soon completely absorbed in accounts of life-styles so extravagant that one writer referred to the eighteenth- and nineteenth-century Creoles as "prince-planters who held court in their castles in the same grand manner as the royal families of Europe." In contrast, there were descriptions of the other early residents of the bayou country, the Cajuns, a number of whom were denounced for having "diluted the purity of their bloodline" by intermarrying with the refugees from Cuba.

One author described this strain of Cajun as having "gone native, developing a society separate from that of their affluent neighbors.

"Much folklore developed," he wrote, "about the renegades who inhabited makeshift shacks along the banks of the river. Though little about their customs was set on paper, it was rumored that they practiced a form of voodoo known as Obeah. The bartering of spells and potions in exchange for material possessions was suspected to be far more common than was generally acknowledged. Many of the Cajun women were extremely beautiful and were supported as mistresses by the Creole landowners."

At this point in my reading, a hand touched my shoulder.

"Nore?" Josie said. "We've been here for hours. Haven't you found the stuff your dad wants yet?"

"We haven't been here for hours at all," I responded. "It's only been fifty minutes. I wish that we *could* stay for hours, these books are so fascinating."

"Some of the accounts are pretty exaggerated," said Josie.

"I don't know how you can make a statement like that," I told her. "I'm sure that these writers spent a great many years doing research." I gathered up the half-dozen volumes that I had chosen as being most interesting. "Let's go see if my father's card is ready so that we can check these out."

When I gave her the name Charles Robbins, the girl at the desk nodded quickly.

"Oh, yes, of course, here's his card right here." She glanced up with a smile. "Did you know that there's a well-known writer by that same name?"

"I certainly do," I said, both proud and embarrassed. "This is that very same person. He's my father."

"Your father wrote *Life in the Fast Lane?*" the girl gasped incredulously. "I can't believe it! A celebrity, right here in Merveille!"

"Well, not *quite* in Merveille," I said. "We live out in the country." And for the next fourteen minutes, I expounded on Dad's writing career for the benefit of the excited librarian and her two assistants, who were summoned up from the dark recesses of the archives to be introduced to "some close relatives of the famous Charles Robbins."

It was, therefore, almost a quarter past eleven before Josie and I, having stopped at the parking lot to deposit our books in the car, entered the Safeway store in search of Lisette. We found her with a loaded shopping cart, already standing in line at the checkout counter.

"What kind of ice cream did you get?" Josie demanded immediately, peering down at the groceries in the cart with sharp-eyed interest. "Oh, great — chocolate! I can't believe you really got that. Yuck, fish again — we just had that last night. Why did you get those dry old Doritos? You know I like potato chips much better."

"I also know that potato chips make your face break out." Lisette turned her attention to me. "How did the book search go? Were you able to find all the books your father wanted?"

"Yes," I said. "There was lots of material that ought to be helpful to him. And do you know what happened when I went to pick up his library card?"

51

I was just getting ready to tell her about the reaction of the librarian, when a voice from the next line over exclaimed, "Lisette? Lisette Bergé, can that possibly be *you?*"

Lisette seemed to freeze for an instant. Then, she turned slowly to face the gray-haired woman who was paying for her groceries at the adjoining register.

"Am I the one to whom you are speaking?" Lisette asked her coolly. "I don't believe that we know each other, do we?"

"Yes, I think — that is — I *did* think —" The woman's smile wavered, and she paused uncertainly. "No, I'm sorry; you're much too young to be the person that I thought you were. I bet, though, that you're related. You must be to look so much alike."

"You're probably thinking about my mother," said Lisette. "Her name was Lisette Bergé, and I was named for her."

"Oh, that explains it then." The woman seemed grateful to have found the solution to the mystery. "I'm Elaine Shannon. I knew your mother way back — oh, it must have been twenty years ago — and if you're her daughter, then I remember you as well. I used to manage a custom dress shop over on River Street. When your mother came in for a fitting, she would bring you with her. You must have been twelve or so at the time — just about the age of this little girl here." She gestured to indicate Josie. "You looked like her too — the same eyes — the exact same coloring."

"This is my daughter, Josephine," Lisette said stiffly. "She does look a lot like I did at her age."

"How time flies!" Elaine Shannon said with a sigh. "It's hard to imagine your pretty, young mother a grandmother. How is she, dear? I'd heard that she had moved up North somewhere."

"She passed away several years ago," said Lisette. Then — "Oh, my goodness!" Turning abruptly, she glanced into her shopping cart with an expression of chagrin. "As usual, I seem to have forgotten something important. It was nice to have met you again, Mrs. Shannon, after so many years. You are sweet to remember my mother with so much affection. Nore, please ask the cashier to go ahead and start ringing things up. I'll be back in one tiny minute."

But she was not.

The cashier did ring up the groceries and then stood fidgeting impatiently while long moments passed and the line behind us grew increasingly longer.

It was not until Elaine Shannon's groceries had all been bagged and the elderly woman had left the store with them that Lisette came rushing back with a cellophane sack in her hand.

"I'm so sorry to have kept you waiting," she told the woman at the register. "I just couldn't seem to find what I was looking for."

Dumbfounded, I stared at the item that she had brought back with her.

It was nothing more nor less than a bag of potato chips.

CHAPTER

6

W E got back to Shadow Grove at slightly past noon. The sun was centered overhead, and its rays slashed down through the canopy of leaves to strike the driveway with sharp bullets of searing light. The warmth of the day had increased to a point that I considered uncomfortable, although it was nothing to compare with the heat that I was to grow accustomed to later in the summer.

The truck labeled "Parlange Roofing Company" was parked in front of the house. Two men — one quite young and the other probably in his forties — were seated in a block of shade under one of the oak trees, munching on sandwiches and washing them down with soda pop. I guessed immediately that the younger man — tall, dark, and shirtless — was the "hunk" that Josie had reacted to in the car that morning.

Lisette gave the horn a sharp beep, and Gabe came grudgingly out to help carry in the groceries. He was friendly enough to me, but cool toward his mother. It was obvious that he was still fuming about not having been permitted to accompany us to Merveille.

While Lisette and I put the food away and started lunch preparations, Josie managed to drift surreptitiously back outside again. When Lisette sent me out to get her, I was not particularly surprised to find her crouched in the grass next to the workmen, chattering away like a triple-tongued parakeet.

Her expression when she saw me approaching was almost enough to send me straight back into the house.

"Lunch is ready," I said, trying to ignore her hostility. "Your mother wants you to come on in now."

"I'm busy," Josie said defiantly. "Besides, I'm not hungry."

"I don't think that's going to go down too well," I told her. "Your mom's got the sandwiches made, and everybody's waiting."

Having had no previous experience in coercing newly-turned-teenagers, I didn't know how to force the issue. I couldn't quite picture myself dragging a kicking, screaming Josie across the lawn to the house.

"You'd better go eat, kid," the older man said in a fatherly tone. "Dave and I have to get back to work soon anyway."

"I'm not hungry," Josie repeated. After a moment's consideration, however, she did get to her feet.

"Before you go," the "hunk" said teasingly, "why don't you introduce us to your pretty friend?"

"Nore isn't my friend," Josie retorted. "She's only my stepsister. I've just barely met her myself."

"How do you do, Stepsister Nore?" The young man

grinned up at me and extended his hand. "I'm Dave Parlange, and this guy, here, is my uncle, Phil. He's the Parlange Roofing Company, and I'm the Parlange Roofing Company's assistant for the summer."

"Hello, Dave," I said, taking his hand and shaking it. "I'm Nore Robbins, and I just got to Shadow Grove yesterday."

"You're from up North," Dave said immediately.

"Is it really that obvious?" I asked, surprised. "How can you tell? I only spoke a couple of words!"

"One of them had an *r* in it. That's a giveaway." He regarded me speculatively. "New York? New Jersey? Maybe Maryland?"

"You were right on the first try," I told him. "I'm from Guilderland, New York. Now, let *me* make a guess. You were born here in Louisiana."

"Right on the button," Dave said. "I've never lived anywhere else. That's going to change in the fall, though — I've got a scholarship to Harvard."

"You have!" I exclaimed. "How marvelous! You're going to love New England. I go to school in Boston, and it's just beautiful there."

"Nore, come *on,*" Josie said impatiently. "You're the one who was making such a big deal out of everybody's waiting for us."

"You're right," I said. "We had better go in. It was nice meeting you, Dave. You, too, Mr. Parlange."

As we headed back to the house, Josie stalked ahead of me with head thrust forward and shoulders set belligerently. I was more amused than upset by the exaggerated display of pique. In the short time I'd been at Shadow Grove, I had already begun to become accustomed to my stepsister's fluctuating moods. The emotional thunderstorms seemed to come and go with little rhyme or reason, and I was willing to bet that this particular one would soon blow over.

I was right. Within minutes after the four of us were seated at the table (Lisette had served Dad's lunch to him in his office, so that he wouldn't have to tear himself away from the typewriter), Josie's aura of gloom had been displaced by her brighter side. As she gobbled her sandwich, her lack of appetite forgotten, she enthusiastically described to Gabe the newly discovered discotheque.

"It's called the Teen Dance Machine," she said. "They've got a big sign up that says they're open every night but Sunday. Why don't we go there tonight and see what it's like?"

"Suits me," Gabe said. "How about you, Nore — want to go dancing?"

"Sure," I said. "It sounds like fun."

"I don't think that would be a very good idea tonight," said Lisette. "Nore has only just arrived, and her father has hardly had a chance to say hello to her. I'm sure that Chuck would like to spend a little time with his daughter before you children go rushing off to some local nightspot."

"Dad won't mind," I said with certainty. "We have the whole summer."

"I want you to wait, Nore." The tone of Lisette's voice left no room for argument. "I'd like to get some information about that 'Dance Machine' place before I give Gabe permission to take you girls there. You don't know what sort of people might frequent an establishment like that. Some of those dance spots are totally inappropriate for teenagers."

"That's crazy!" exclaimed Josie. "It's called the *Teen Dance Machine*! It wouldn't have that name if it weren't an under-twenty-one club."

"We'll discuss this later," said her mother. "Let's not argue over lunch, dear."

"You're mean!" Josie exploded. "You're just plain mean! You never want us to do anything!"

"I said *later,* Jo," Lisette repeated quietly.

" 'Later' — 'later' — it's always 'later'! I'm sick of 'later'! What's the sense of living if we can't have some fun right *now?*"

Shoving back her chair so hard that she almost tipped it over, Josie jumped up from the table and bolted from the room.

Lisette sighed. "Once again, I apologize for my daughter, Nore. I hate for you to have to keep witnessing scenes like this one, but I can't start giving in to Josie when she throws these tantrums. She's right at that age when nothing is less than a crisis to her. After she's calmed down a bit, I'll go up and see if I can reason with her."

She paused, shifted mental gears, and then asked brightly, "Who will have another sandwich? You're ready for one, aren't you, Gabe? You've always been a two-sandwich boy. Now, tell me, Nore, which books did you find for your father?"

So, I described the books that I had checked out of the library. Lisette seemed to be familiar with almost all of them and commented knowledgeably on both the contents and the authors. The remainder of the lunch hour passed pleasantly enough, and, although Gabe did not take much part in the conversation, he did not seem to be especially upset about the fact that our half-formed plan for the evening had been aborted.

When the meal was over, Lisette suggested that we all go upstairs and "take a midday lie-down."

"That's a custom here in the South," she explained to me. "We get up early to take advantage of the cool of the summer mornings and then take siestas in the middle of the day to avoid the heat."

When the idea was proposed it sounded reasonable enough. Once ensconced in my room, however, I found napping impossible. Although I'd been up since dawn, I wasn't the least bit drowsy. The pounding of the workmen on the roof shattered the noonday quiet, and the moment I lay down on the bed, my mind started seething with questions about this family that my father's marriage had made me an inadvertent part of.

The exchange at the breakfast table still disturbed me. Something had happened there, something not obvious enough for me to be able to pinpoint, but meaningful nevertheless. And what about the scene that morning at the supermarket? Why had Lisette reacted so strangely to the encounter with her late mother's dressmaker? It was not surprising that she would not have recognized the woman — twenty years was a long time to remember anyone — but I could see no reason for her response to have been so icy. And the potato chips! Lisette had told Josie that she would not buy them. It was obvious that the "important errand" that had taken her back into the store so hastily had been manufactured to escape further conversation with Elaine Shannon.

That wasn't all that bothered me either. Mrs. Shannon had called my stepmother Lisette Bergé, a name that, Lisette had tried to explain, had also been her mother's. Yet Bergé had been not Lisette's maiden name, but the name that she had acquired through her previous marriage.

The room was unbearably close, and my body was sticky

with perspiration. When I had first come upstairs, I had pulled shut the louvers of the French doors in an effort to block out the sunlight. Now, realizing my mistake, I got up from the bed and threw both the front and side doors open to the balcony.

No stir of breeze rewarded this effort. Beyond the wooden railing, the great, green heads of the oak trees hung motionless in the still air. In the driveway below, the gleaming metallic roof of the Parlange truck threw off shimmering waves of heat, and in the garden to the east, the rosebushes seemed to sag wearily beneath their overload of drooping blossoms.

The combination of the midday heat and the dry textured sandwich I had eaten at lunchtime was making me terribly thirsty. Turning away from the balcony, I went back across the room and opened the door to the hall. As soon as I stepped out into the hallway, I became conscious of the low hum of voices in the adjoining room. True to her word, Lisette had apparently gone in to talk with Josie.

I was halfway across the hall, en route to the bathroom, when my stepsister's voice rose suddenly in high-pitched accusation.

"— because of *Nore!*" she exclaimed. "It's just not fair!"

"Hush," Lisette said. "Hush now, Jo. You know better than that."

Her voice dropped, and the rest of the words were lost to me.

I continued on into the bathroom and ran a glass full of water. I felt oddly shaken, both by the jolt of hearing my name shouted out so unexpectedly and by the emotion with which it had been uttered. What I had heard in Josie's voice had not been the resentful whine of a complaining teenager. It had been a cry of very real anguish.

I drank the water slowly and then, with the empty glass still clutched in my hand, went back out into the hall. The murmur of voices continued in the room across from me, and though I couldn't be certain, I thought that I again heard my name.

For a long time I stood immobile, staring at the closed door. Then I did something that it embarrasses me to admit to. I lifted the bathroom water glass to the door of Josie's bedroom and held its open end tight against the wooden panel. Then, I pressed my ear to the bottom of the glass.

The technique that I had once read about did actually work. The sound in the room beyond the door was tremendously magnified.

It was Lisette who was speaking.

"— keep them apart as much as possible," she was saying. "Your brother is obviously very much attracted to her."

"You can't hope to keep them apart," Josie objected. "Both of them *live* here. There's no way to keep them from seeing each other."

"I *also* live here," her mother reminded her. "At Shadow Grove, *I* am the one in control of things. Gabe knows that and, while he may not like it, he has no choice but to accept it. They will see each other here, yes, but under my supervision. In a dating situation, the atmosphere would be different. Things could get out of hand very quickly."

"But, how, at a disco —"

"You must trust me," said Lisette. "I do know what's best for us."

"How can you say that!" Jose fired back angrily. "*You* got us into this! *You* made the deal! You never asked our advice or our permission! It was bad enough for the boys, but for *me* —"

"I know," Lisette said softly. "Josie, I do know, and, believe me, I'm sorry. This situation is in a way worse for me than for anyone. If I had it to do again, I would certainly do it differently. But, I didn't think. I was young — I was furious — my emotions were out of control. I did what I thought would be the right thing for the four of us."

"But, it *wasn't!*" Josie was crying now. "We can't go on like this, Maman! We've got to get some fun out of life! Please, let us go dancing!"

"No," Lisette said regretfully. "Please, trust me, dear. I made one bad mistake, but I don't intend to make another. If a romance should develop between Gabe and Chuck's daughter, it could destroy everything. Gabe might even tell her —"

"He wouldn't do that!"

"Nore Robbins is a danger." Lisette's voice was low, but the glass brought the words to my ear with the precision of a telephone receiver. "She is by far the worst threat that we have ever had to face."

"Why?" Josie asked her. "Just tell me, *why* is Nore such a threat? Because Gabe likes her? Gabe's liked lots of girls! You've never objected before when he got hung up on somebody. We all of us know how those romances of his have to end."

"This is different," said Lisette, "because Nore is Chuck's daughter. She is part of the package that Gabe will soon have to deal with. But there may be even more of a problem than that, Jo. Maybe it's something to worry about, or maybe it isn't; there's no way yet to be certain what effect this may have on things. The fact is, though, that with Nore Robbins, for the first time since all this started, we are involved with someone who has an uncanny awareness of *time.*"

CHAPTER
7

I WAS far too ashamed of the way in which I had eavesdropped on that conversation to have even considered repeating it to my father. I have wondered since what his reaction would have been if I had. It was still so early. The friction between us had not yet developed. Might he have believed me then, if I had told him the things that I had overheard, and, if so, would they have made any sort of sense to him?

I doubt that they would have, for they certainly didn't to me. Safely back in my room, with the hall door closed behind me, I sat down on the bed and let the strange dialogue play back through my mind. *"You* made the deal!" What deal could Josie have been talking about? "Nore Robbins is a danger." That was ridiculous. How could a seventeen-year-old girl be a danger to anybody? The "awareness of time" that Lisette had referred to was of no importance to anybody except to me, for whom it was significant only because it meant that I didn't have to wear a watch.

Perhaps I had heard things incorrectly, I told myself. It was possible — no, it was *probable* — that the drinking glass had distorted the voices behind Josie's door. What Lisette had said, quite likely, had been, "Nore Robbins is a *stranger*" — a stranger whose presence might threaten her control over her son.

In retrospect, I realize that the more I sifted through the sands of that strange conversation, the more the tiny grains of meaning slid away from me. At last, exhausted from the effort, I stretched out on the bed, determined to take Lisette's suggestion to take a "siesta." The activity on the roof had now ceased, and before long I heard the engine of the Parlange truck come to life in the driveway. That sound receded with increasing distance and was replaced at last by silence, broken only by the drone of cicadas singing their naptime songs in the trees beyond the open doors to the balcony. I did manage to nap a bit, though my mind must have kept on rationalizing while I was dozing, because when I opened my eyes again, the exchange between Lisette and Josie had taken on the semblance of a half-remembered dream. The one fact that did remain sharp in my mind was the one that I *wanted* to hold there — that his mother felt that Gabe was attracted to me.

At dinner that night I was so aware of Gabe's presence that I could scarcely bring myself to look across at him. I had found him attractive at first meeting, and the possibility that this feeling might be reciprocated was enough to make me both exhilarated and nervous. The high, arched cheekbones that stood out like wings beneath the taut, tanned skin; the sensitive mouth; the deep-set eyes, sometimes shadowed and thoughtful, sometimes twinkling with laughter, all seemed suddenly incredibly exciting.

As often happened when he was enthused about a new writing project, Dad was monopolizing the conversation. Lisette sat, listening in fascination, as he went over every detail of the scene that he had worked on that afternoon. Under the assumption that everyone's attention was directed toward my father, I permitted myself a quick glance in Gabe's direction. I was startled to find that his eyes were waiting for mine.

Our gaze locked into place, and I felt my cheeks growing hot. To cover my embarrassment, I groped blindly for my water glass. My hand slid past it and almost knocked it over.

Keeping a deadpan expression, Gabe let one eyelid drop in an exaggerated wink. Josie, who was seated next to him, raised her napkin to her mouth in an attempt to muffle a giggle. As I glanced back and forth between brother and sister, I saw that both sets of eyes were dancing with light that was more than a simple reflection of flames from the dinner candles. It seemed suddenly to me that the two of them were enjoying an amusing secret that I was being silently invited to share.

"Did you get a nap today?" Gabe asked me softly.

"A nap?"

"I know Maman sent you upstairs to take one. She's a great one for that sort of thing." His voice dropped even lower, now almost a whisper. "The problem is, though, that I don't think she took a nap herself. I have this weird feeling that she and your father may get sleepy quite early tonight. What do you think, Josie?"

"I think it'll be lullaby time along about nine-thirty." This time Josie's giggle could not be stifled, but came bubbling out in a kind of hiccough.

Her mother turned to frown at her.

"What in the world are you whispering about, Jo? If it's all that funny, why don't you share it with the rest of us?"

"We're telling dirty jokes," Josie said blandly. "We didn't think that you'd be interested in hearing them."

"Well, you were right about that," said Lisette. "I don't want to hear them, and *you* don't need to tell them, especially not at the dinner table. If you ever tried listening, for a change, instead of talking, you might learn something interesting. How many people have the chance to know the plot of a book before it has even been written?"

For the remainder of the meal, we listened to Dad's discourse on his new novel, and it wasn't until dinner was over that he had finally managed to talk himself out. Then, while Gabe served the adults after-dinner drinks in the courtyard, Josie and I cleared the table and loaded the dishwasher. By the time that we were finished in the kitchen and could join the family outside, their conversation had become focused on other subjects.

"— to bring a crew out here to put in the telephone," Lisette said saying, as Josie and I came out onto the patio. "We're out so far from town, they'll have to put in a special line. It may take them a while to get this sort of project going."

"What I don't understand is why you didn't have it done long ago," said Dad. "In this day and age, how can anybody live without a phone?"

"I've never missed it," said Lisette. "A telephone's a luxury that simply never struck me as particularly important. I'm not a person who gets involved in many social activities. Not putting in a phone meant one less intrusion on our privacy."

"You and your precious privacy!" The exasperation in

Dad's voice was tempered by affection. "Well, I can't afford that luxury. My agent and editors need to be able to reach me. Besides, I don't think it's safe to be so out of touch with people. What if we had an emergency out here and needed to get help? What if one of the kids got hurt and we had to call an ambulance?"

"Please, Chuck, don't lecture me. You're right, I know. I told you, I've got our name on the mile-long waiting list. The telephone company will get to us as soon as they can." Lisette shielded her mouth to cover a yawn. "I don't know why I'm suddenly so sleepy. I'm embarrassed to say, I can hardly keep my eyes open."

"I'm not so bright-eyed myself," Dad admitted a bit sheepishly. "It's been so long since I've spent a full day writing that I'd almost forgotten how draining it could be. Why don't we make an early night of it?"

"I won't give you any argument about that." Lisette glanced across at me. "Nore, you must be exhausted, you were up so early. Aren't you about ready to turn in, too?"

"Not really —" I started to say, but Gabe interrupted me.

"Why don't we all of us call it a night? I've got some reading to do. Now that I've got a famous author for a stepfather, I need to start reading novels."

"I'm going to go up to my room and play records," announced Josie.

So, although I was not feeling in the slightest bit sleepy, I found myself leaving the moonlit courtyard with the others. As I mounted the stairs with the rest of them, I couldn't help but think how strange it was that Gabe and Josie had predicted this early retirement hour.

We bid each other goodnight in the upstairs hallway. Dad gave me a quick kiss on the cheek, but his eyes were on Li-

sette. Then we split forces to head for our respective bedrooms.

"Don't go to bed yet," Josie whispered to me as we
walked together down the hall. "I know you're not any
sleepier than I am."

"What do you mean?" I asked her. "What else is there to
do?"

"We can go to the disco."

"Go *where?*" I regarded her incredulously. "But, your
mother told us —"

"Give our folks fifteen minutes, and they'll be out for the
count. Neither one will know another thing until morning."
Josie flashed me a mischievous grin. "Go on into your room
and wait. I'll check things out with Gabe, and then I'll be
back for you."

Too surprised to question her further, I did as directed.
Once I was in my bedroom, however, I felt both foolish and
bewildered. Was this some sort of joke, or was Josie serious?
Did she actually expect to be able to pull off a stunt like this?

I sat down on the edge of the bed to await further devel-
opments. Ten minutes passed — which became fifteen —
then twenty — then twenty-two. Then, just as I was making
the decision to get into bed and read myself to sleep, there
was a light rap on my door. When I opened it, I found Josie
standing in the hallway. She was dressed in skintight jeans
and a V-neck shirt that hung open to a point halfway down
her chest. Her cheeks were bright with rouge, and her lashes
so lathered with mascara that they adhered to each other to
form one solid layer of sediment.

"Are you ready?" she whispered. "Gabe's getting the keys
out of the Maman's purse. He's going to meet us out front
with the car in a minute."

"Oh, Josie, I really don't know about this," I said doubtfully. "Your mother *did* tell us —"

"Nore, please?" Josie said beseechingly. "Gabe won't take me out dancing unless you come too. He doesn't want to go anyplace like this with only his sister."

"You want to go so badly?"

"It'll be a blast, Nore!" Josie's eyes were shining. "They've got this great huge video screen and all the latest rock tapes. There's this disk jockey guy who'll play anything you want him to. All the kids from Merveille go there. It's where all the action is."

"How do you know all this?" I asked her. "It wasn't on that sign we saw."

"Dave told me," said Josie. "You know, Dave, that guy with the roofing company? He said it's a really cool place. He goes there all the time."

"I see," I said softly, gazing down into her small, hopeful face, so painfully vulnerable beneath its ridiculous clown mask of makeup. I *did* see — exactly. I had been thirteen once myself. "All right, Jo, I'll go with you. But, just this once. I'm not going to make a business of sneaking out like this."

"Nore, thanks! You're terrific!" Josie threw her arms around me in an impulsive hug. The embrace was so out of character and took me so by surprise that I was nearly toppled over. "It'll be fun, you'll see! We're going to have a great time!"

"I hope so," I said, "because I don't feel good about this, Josie. I really do hope that the evening turns out to be worth it."

I would like to be able to say that my decision was altruistic and I was agreeing to sneak out that night just because of Josie. That's partially true, of course. I did feel sympathy for my young stepsister; I could remember all too well my own first crush on an inaccessible boy. I will have to admit, though, that I had another motive as well. I wanted a date — a real, away-from-Shadow-Grove date — with Gabe Bergé. I wanted — well, all right, I'll come right straight out and say it — I wanted to spite Lisette. And I wanted to be kissed by her son.

So, shivering slightly with nervous anticipation, I crept with Josie down the hall and down the stairs and out into the magic of the flower-scented night.

Lisette's Monte Carlo was in front of the house with the motor running, and the door on the passenger's side was standing open. Josie shoved the front seat forward so she could scramble into the back, and Gabe raised a hand from the steering wheel in a gesture of greeting.

"I knew you'd come!" he said triumphantly as I shoved the seat back into place and climbed in next to him. His face, illuminated by moonlight, seemed to throw off its own strange radiance as though it were lit from within as well as from above. "The first moment I saw you, I knew you were my kind of girl!"

"I've got to be crazy to be doing this," I told him, pulling the door closed as carefully as I could in the hope that it would make a click rather than a slamming sound. "If your mother wakes up and checks on us —"

"She won't do that," said Josie. "Maman never wakes up when she's had the sleepytime anisette."

"She drank anisette last night, too," I reminded her. "That didn't make her sleepy. She and my dad were up long past the time that I went to bed."

"What they drank last night was from the bottle in the

pantry," said Josie. "Tonight Gabe poured their drinks from the bottle in his room."

"From his room?" I repeated skeptically. "Do you mean there are two different bottles?"

"Josie and I like to refer to them as the 'regular' and the 'sleepytime,' " said Gabe. "One's for ordinary nights, and one's for special nights like this one." There was a note in his voice that made me think that he might be smiling, but we were now moving down the shadowy driveway, and I could no longer see the expression on his face.

When he pulled through the gate out onto the road, however, the moonlight came bursting upon us like a silver spotlight.

Gabe turned to grin across at me. "Well, we made it! Out of the cobwebs of Shadow Grove and into the *now!*"

"And off to the Dance Machine!" crowed Josie.

"Yes, off to the Dance Machine!" This was a whole different Gabe from the one I was used to seeing. "Get over here, Nore!" he commanded with mock ferocity. "Tonight we're going to forget all the 'stepbrother' stuff. If you've got a hometown boyfriend, I don't want to know about him."

Willingly, I slid across to sit close beside him.

"I don't have a boyfriend," I said. "At least, not anyone serious. The boys I dated in Guilderland were just good buddies."

Gabe's arm slipped down and tightened around my shoulders, and I felt those electric currents run all the way through me.

It was the beginning of a night that I would always remember.

It was also, in certain ways, the beginning of the end.

CHAPTER

❖ 8 ❖

IT was almost ten-thirty by the time we got to Merveille. As we cruised through the center of town, the place seemed so empty that I began to wonder if we had made a mistake in coming. There was no one on the sidewalks, and the row of storefronts facing out upon the main street were either totally dark or lit dimly from the back. The only evidence of life was a few cars parked in front of the movie theater and some people munching hamburgers behind the window of McDonald's.

As we approached the Teen Dance Machine, however, the atmosphere changed abruptly. We were still a full block away when the blare of rock music came rolling down the street to meet us, and when we pulled into the lot at the side of the building, there were enough cars assembled there so that Gabe had difficulty finding a parking slot.

"We close at twelve on weeknights," the man at the register told us as he accepted our admission fees. "That's not going to allow you kids much time here."

72

"That's okay," Gabe told him. "We really just want to see what the place is like. Next time we'll get here earlier."

"Suit yourself," the man said with a shrug. "It's your money."

He stamped the back of Gabe's hand with the date in India ink and then did the same to mine.

When Josie, in turn, extended her hand, he hestitated.

"This is a teen club, kid," he said suspiciously. "You don't look more than twelve to me."

"Are you crazy!" Josie exclaimed indignantly. "I'm as teenage as anybody!"

The man regarded her skeptically. "How about showing me your student I.D.?"

"I don't have one," said Josie. "I don't go to school here. I've been living in Chicago."

"The schools in Chicago don't give out student I.D. cards?"

"Not the school I went to," Josie told him.

"I'm her brother," Gabe interjected. "I'll vouch for her. She's thirteen and a half."

"Well, okay," the man said reluctantly. "But, she's your responsibility. Keep an eye on her and see that she doesn't get hassled."

"Nobody has to take care of me," snapped Josie. "I've been to discos a whole lot wilder than this one."

I, myself, could not have made that statement. Although I'd been to plenty of school dances, the crowd I'd run with back in Guilderland had not been in the habit of frequenting dance halls, and my year in a restrictive New England boarding school had certainly not provided any such experiences. To me, the Teen Dance Machine was a new adventure, and within seconds my senses were reeling with the impact of flashing lights and ear-shattering music. The ceil-

73

ing of the cavernous room was hung with spinning mirrors that threw whirling rainbows down upon the gyrating teenagers below it. At the room's far end, on a huge, rectangular video screen, the images of rock stars writhed and twisted right along with the dancers to the crashing rhythm of recorded sound.

"Dance with me, Gabe?" Josie pleaded eagerly.

"Later, kid," Gabe told her, not unkindly. "This first one's with Nore."

Grabbing my hand, he pulled me out onto the dance floor. For one crazy moment, as people closed in on all sides of us, my mind flew back to Josie's remark about the fire in the Ringling circus tent when she "almost got trampled to death" in a mad stampede. An instant later, however, that thought and all others were forgotten as Gabe's arm came around me and I gave myself up to the pounding beat of the music.

Time passed; I don't know how much. My time sense was overpowered that night by my other senses. The flash of lights and the intensity of sound, combined with the immediacy of Gabe's presence — the grip of his hands on mine, the heat of his body, the strange sense of intimacy, as though we two formed our own private island in a churning human sea — were too overwhelming to allow for any further sensations. Gabe danced with the grace of a jungle cat, his lithe body surprisingly strong and under perfect control. We were so close in height that our faces were on the same level, and as he spun me away and then brought me whipping back to him, I could see my reflection in the dark twin mirrors of his eyes.

When the music came to an end, he pulled me to him. For a moment, I was held so tightly against his chest that I could feel the thud of his heartbeat as though it were my own.

74

Then, just as abruptly, he released me.

"You can dance!" he said approvingly. "I mean, *really* dance!"

"So — can — you!" I gasped, breathless as much from his nearness as from physical exertion. "Do you see Josie anywhere? We probably shouldn't have left her so long by herself."

"She wasn't by herself. She was out on the dance floor when we were." He scanned the milling crowd. "Oh — there she is, over there. She's latched onto the Incredible Hulk from the roofing company."

Following his gaze, I saw a radiant Josie headed toward us, her hand clamped firmly onto the arm of Dave Parlange.

"Look who I found!" she announced triumphantly as they came up beside us. "We were out there dancing! Did you see us?"

"Gabe did, but I missed it." I couldn't help smiling at the mental picture of such an unlikely combination of dance partners. Dave had to be over six feet tall, and tiny Josie, in her provocative outfit and exotic makeup, looked like nothing so much as a small girl dressed for a costume party.

"Hi, Dave!" I said. "Have you met Gabe Bergé, Josie's brother?"

"I don't think so," Dave said, extending his hand. "Good to meet you, Gabe."

"Same here," Gabe said with a minimum of enthusiasm. He gave Dave's hand a perfunctory shake. "I hear that you guys finished up with the roof today."

"At long last," Dave said good-naturedly. "That was one big job! I'm sure you're not going to miss all that banging over your heads." He turned to Josie. "What do you say, kid? Ready for another round?"

75

"Oh, yes!" Josie's eyes were shining. "See, Nore, wasn't I right? I told you we'd have a blast here, and Maman won't ever have to know."

"Gabe," I said, as Josie and Dave moved out of earshot, "I want to know about this 'sleepytime' anisette you gave our parents. It scares me to think of doping people up like that. Are you sure the stuff that's in it isn't going to hurt them?"

"Of course I'm sure," Gabe said. "We've been doing this for years, Nore. It's not a prescription drug, it's just some herbs."

"Herbs?" I repeated. "You mean like mint leaves or oregano? How can something that grows in the garden put people to sleep?"

"There are plenty of herbs in the world that you've probably never heard of," Gabe said. "Pasote, tartago, bilda, xanthan and anamu for starters. The right combinations can do all sorts of things to people. The secret is, you have to know how to use them."

"Where did you get the herbs for the anisette?" I asked him skeptically.

"From one of the Cajun 'witch girls,' " Gabe said with a grin. "A pretty girl, too, but not quite as pretty as you are."

"Was she your girlfriend?" I asked, trying to make the question sound casual.

"I guess you could say that," Gabe said. "That was a long time ago, though. I don't remember too much about Felicité, except that she was pretty and lived in a cottage over by the river. She had this herb garden out behind it, and she gave me some cuttings. I planted them at Shadow Grove."

"It couldn't have been *that* long ago," I objected. "You're only seventeen now. What did you do, start dating when you were in nursery school?"

76

"I was a very precocious child," Gabe told me blandly. "And — talk about precocious — here comes my baby sister with her muscle-headed roofer friend. The guy looks totally bushed, and the song isn't even over yet. I think Jo's danced him straight through the floor."

"Dave may be big," I said, "but he's certainly no 'muscle-head.' He's been accepted at Harvard, and he's even got a scholarship."

"No kidding!" Gabe said. "Well, I've heard that those Ivy League schools like to flaunt their token minority students. Maybe they've accepted Parlange as their 'token roofer.' If you ask me —"

He broke off the sentence as Josie came rushing up to us with Dave trailing wearily along behind her.

"Come dance with me, Gabe?" she pleaded, grabbing her brother's hand. "Dave's tired, and I'm not, and it's almost twelve already. This place is going to close in just a few minutes."

"And you want to make good use of every one of them, is that it?" Gabe asked teasingly.

"Yes, of course! It's a special evening, and Nore's had *her* turn!"

"Go ahead, Gabe," I said, laughing. "I'm all danced out. I want to see which of the two of you is going to drop first."

"It won't be Josie; you can bet on that," Dave commented wryly, as we watched her drag Gabe out onto the dance floor. "That little girl's got more energy than a steam engine. What do you guys feed her, anyway — pep pills à la mode?"

"Sugar Pops," I told him, "and gumbo and potato chips. Actually, she's not always this hyper. She's just all souped up tonight and excited about being here."

"She's a funny kid," Dave said. "There's something about her —" The end of his sentence was drowned out by the blare of the music.

"What do you mean?" I asked him, leaning closer. " 'Funny,' how?"

"I don't know exactly," he said. "I've been trying to figure it out. The first day my uncle Phil and I started working at Shadow Grove, she came out to talk to us. She seemed like a nice kid — kind of lonely and at loose ends — I didn't mind visiting during our lunch break. My sister Marcy's an eighth grader, so I'm used to girls that age. But, Josie would say things — really weird things —"

"Like what?" I asked.

"Well, like for instance, she asked me how tall I was. When I told her, she said, 'My brother would give anything to be six foot one.' I said, 'Who knows? Maybe he will be. I grew a full three inches my senior year in high school.' And Josie said, 'That won't happen to poor Gabe. He's stuck where he is.' "

"She was just being silly," I said. "I think she says dumb things sometimes just to get attention."

"All kids do that," Dave acknowledged. "Even Marcy does sometimes. But this thing with Josie was different. It was like the statement just sort of popped out without her knowing it was going to. Then, when she realized what she'd said, she got all flustered and tried to make a joke of it."

"That *is* odd," I admitted.

"Well, maybe I'm making too much out of it." He paused, then smiled. "Hey, not to change the subject, but how long are you here for? In the state, I mean, not here at the Dance Machine. Is it just for a short visit or for the whole summer?"

"For the summer," I said. "It's a 'get-acquainted' visit with my stepfamily."

"Then, would it be all right if I called you sometime? Maybe we could go to a movie or something."

"That would be nice," I said. "The problem is, though, we haven't got a telephone."

"How about my stopping by if I'm out in your area?"

"When would you ever be 'out in our area'?" I asked teasingly. "According to Josie, Shadow Grove's a million miles from nowhere."

"Maybe I can come up with an errand of some kind to bring me out there," Dave said. "Josie tells me that you're having a pool put in. Don't you think it would be useful to have it roofed over?"

"It certainly would," I responded, matching his solemn tone. "I don't swim, so I wouldn't get much use out of it myself, but it would keep the others dry if they wanted to swim when it was raining." Unable to keep up the game, I started to laugh. "Do come out if you can. We'd all be glad to see you."

Especially Josie, I added silently, picturing her ecstasy if Dave Parlange were to suddenly appear on the doorstep. For my own part, I wasn't too sure that I was ready yet to get into a round of summer dating. Before I started going out with other people, I wanted to see if what I felt happening between Gabe and me was going to escalate into a full-fledged romance.

As we had been warned by the manager, the Teen Dance Machine closed down exactly at midnight and there was a noisy mass exodus out to the crowded parking lot. "See you soon, guys," Dave said casually as we headed off in opposite directions to locate our cars. The Monte Carlo was parked

79

safely where we had left it — it had not, in Cinderella style, turned into a pumpkin — and Gabe, Josie and I piled into it, all three of us suddenly gone quiet, drained and exhausted by the high tempo of the evening.

It wasn't until we had left the town of Merveille behind us and were out on the highway that Gabe seemed abruptly to zero in on Dave's parting remark. When he did, his reaction was unexpected.

"What did Parlange mean by that comment about 'seeing us soon'?" The tone of his voice made the question more of an accusation than a query. "The roofing's been completed. There's no reason why we should ever have to see that guy again."

I was sitting with my eyes closed, relaxed and almost dozing, enjoying the pleasant ache of tired muscles and the soothing rush of soft air as it washed in against my face through the open window.

"Dave asked me if he could some visit us out at Shadow Grove," I said drowsily. "I told him that, of course, we'd be happy to see him."

"You told him that, without asking the rest of us first?" Gabe's formerly jubilant mood seemed to have vanished completely. "Don't you think that was pretty presumptuous of you?"

"No, I don't," I said, surprised and hurt by the question. "I didn't think I needed permission to ask someone over. Your mother told me herself that I was to consider Shadow Grove my home. In my own home, I should be free to invite the guests I want."

"Don't be silly about this, Gabe," said Josie, leaning forward in the backseat to add her two cents' worth to the conversation. "You know how much I want to see Dave

80

again. If Nore *had* asked us, I would have said, 'Wow-ee! Terrific!' "

"I'm sure you would have," said her brother. "You've got another one of your king-sized crushes, and you're just not thinking straight. This guy is college age. You don't really believe that it would be you he'd be coming to see, do you?"

"Well, sure," said Josie. "Who else would it be? I'm the one who's his friend. He hardly knows the rest of you."

"You're living in a dream world, Jo," Gabe said, with what seemed to me an inappropriate show of bitterness. "You should know by this time that this sort of thing can't work. It hasn't before, and it won't now. It won't in the future either, not in all of the next million years."

In a sudden, startling display of unprovoked anger, he slammed his foot down on the accelerator, and the car leapt forward with a jolting burst of speed. With his right foot pressing the gas pedal flat against the floorboards, Gabe gripped the steering wheel tightly with both hands and glared out through the front windshield at the long strip of empty road unwinding ahead of us.

Sliding low in my seat, I watched nervously as the needle crept higher and higher on the gauge of the speedometer. Beyond the side windows, the moonlit shapes of trees shot past us at increasing speed until they melded into an indistinguishable blur.

"Gabe —" I began shakily, unable to believe that this could really be happening. My voice was lost in the rush of wind past the windows.

"Gabe, slow down!" Josie yelled at the top of her lungs. "You're scaring me! What are you trying to do, get us all killed?"

"Why not?" Gabe shouted back at her. "We've none of us

died before! It would be an exciting experience, better even than disco!"

"Don't joke about things like that!" Josie commanded. "You're not being funny, Gabe. Please, slow down! You just can't *do* this to us!"

"Oh, can't I?" Gabe asked matter-of-factly. "You've had your evening of dancing. That's what you wanted, wasn't it? Now, here you are, complaining because I want to have a good time too. I like to drive fast; it gets the adrenaline flowing. What's the use of living if you can't do the things you enjoy?"

"You're sounding just like Louis!" Josie cried miserably.

"So, maybe I *am* like Louis, or maybe I'd like to be! Lou had guts! He did things his way and accepted the consequences!"

"Gabe, stop this! Have you gone crazy?" I tried to shriek out the words, but my voice had shrunken with terror, and the plea that emerged was no more than a strangled whimper. "I don't know what this is all about — but, please, Gabe — please —"

At that point, something happened that, I now feel certain, saved our lives that night. The whine of the wind was joined by another, shriller sound — the familiar wail of a siren, growing steadily louder.

"It's a police car!" Josie twisted in her seat to look back through the rear window. "Gabe, you're going to have to pull over! He's right behind us!"

"A cop?" Gabe said blankly. "Where could a cop have come from? I didn't think anybody ever patrolled out here by the river."

"Thank God, you were wrong!" I said, regaining control of my voice as relief surged through me. When I felt the speed of the car beginning to lessen, my terror was replaced by anger. "I hope he fines you a fortune! I hope that he —"

"Do you have your driver's license with you?" Gabe asked me.

His voice was calm and pleasant. I turned to stare at him. This was the old Gabe, speaking — the Gabe who had walked with me by the pond that morning, who had given me a tour of the slave quarters, who had laughed and joked with me at dinner. The wild-eyed young man of a moment ago had vanished. I could not believe the suddenness of the transformation.

"Do you?" he prodded.

"Yes, of course," I said. "It's in my wallet."

"Then, change seats with me when we stop. There's no time for arguing —" as my mouth popped open in automatic protest. "Don't worry, I'll finance the fine, but you've got to help me. If I'm nailed as the driver tonight, there's going to be hell to pay."

"What do you mean?" I asked in bewilderment. "Don't *you* have a license?"

"Not any longer," Gabe said. "It expired, and there was a problem about renewing it. I'll explain the whole thing later. Nore, you've got to come through for me! I know you're mad right now, but this is terribly important."

The most incredible part of this story is that I did what he commanded. As Gabe brought the car to a rolling stop on the shoulder of the road, I allowed him to haul me across his lap and place me in the driver's seat. He, himself, slid across to the passenger's side, so that by the time the patrolman came up to the car, it was I who was situated behind the wheel.

The policeman was a grandfatherly man with a shock of

thick, gray hair and a face well-grooved with smile lines. He was not smiling now.

"I booked you at almost ninety," he told me icily, as he watched me fumble through my wallet to locate my license. "Do you see that big tree sticking out in the curve of the road up ahead? Back at the station, we call that Killer Oak. A half-dozen people have lost their lives plowing into that. What were you kids trying to do, commit triple suicide?"

My mind echoed the question — what *had* Gabe been trying to do? What possible reason could there have been for his crazy behavior? He had not been drinking; had not done drugs; had not even, as far as I could see, had anything happen to him that night that might reasonably have been expected to have made him angry. Obviously, he had not been happy about my having invited Dave over, but that, alone, should not have evoked such a violent reaction.

As the policeman wrote out a ticket, I glanced surreptitiously across at the young man next to me. His head was bent, and his face was lost in shadows.

"I'll explain the whole thing later," he had assured me. Well, I certainly meant to insist that he keep his word.

CHAPTER

9

ALTHOUGH I did not know it then, my initial days at Shadow Grove were more important than the sum of the events that filled them. They were my initiation to the strangeness of my new situation and my introduction to the further strangeness that was soon to follow.

As life settled into place and I became used to the regime there, what had, at first, seemed noteworthy began to seem commonplace to me. There was a regular routine to which I quickly became accustomed. I grew used to waking to the rosy light of a southern dawn and to watching the sunrise fade from two sections of sky. I settled into the routine of taking an early stroll about the grounds, although Gabe was never again to be a part of such occasions. I would see him, sometimes, engaged in his morning running, and he would smile and wave in greeting as he passed me, but he never stopped to talk.

The truth of it is that during those particular weeks, Gabe

didn't talk to me much at all. It was as though the romantic attraction that had initially flared between us had been killed on that mad drive back from Merveille.

I don't mean to imply that he totally stopped speaking. The morning after our traumatic evening, he apologized profusely for having been "so dumb and reckless" and for having given his sister and me such a terrible scare. He paid me the money to cover the fine for speeding and even volunteered to carry the preaddressed envelope the policeman had given me down to the road to hand in person to the mailman. Beyond that point, he was polite and pleasant when we were together as a family, but on all other occasions he kept his distance, both physically and emotionally.

When I pressed him on the subject of his driver's license, he was, at once, both vague and seemingly candid.

"I let it lapse while we were living in Chicago," he told me. "I'm sure that by this time you've noticed what a worrywart my mother is. She was so uptight about my driving in city traffic that I never got to use the car, so it just didn't seem important to get my license renewed."

"You could have had it done in the months since you got back," I said. "It can't be all that difficult a procedure."

"You wouldn't think so," Gabe agreed, "but it's turned out to be a hassle. I've had to send to Baton Rouge for a certified copy of my birth certificate, and for some weird reason, I'm having a hell of a time getting it. The original is there someplace, of course, but there's some sort of mess-up in the records department, and they can't seem to locate it. They're making a search, but, in the meantime, I'm not supposed to drive."

And so the slow-paced days of summer slid one into another, indistinguishable except for Wednesdays, which were the days when Lisette's cleaning girl came. After my step-mother's dinner-table dissertation on the Cajuns and the exotic descriptions I'd read in the books in the library, I have to admit to experiencing a slight feeling of disappointment when Celina arrived that first Wednesday, dressed in a Mickey Mouse T-shirt and blue jeans, with a Walkman cassette player attached to her belt. A quiet, gentle-faced girl, not much older than I, she wore her long brown hair pulled back in a ponytail and worked to the accompaniment of hard rock channeled to her through earphones. Although I did recall Lisette's statement that "the strain has been watered down," I was still unprepared to meet someone so pleasant and ordinary.

As the summer progressed, so did the heat. I could literally feel it increasing from one day to the next. By the third week of June, the promise of it was there awaiting me before I opened my eyes in the morning, and by nine the total weight of it was already starting to descend upon us. The midday siesta became not only acceptable to me, but a necessary part of each day, and evenings did not drop to a temperature that I considered comfortable until several hours after the sun had disappeared behind the oak trees.

What did we do with ourselves during those long, drifting days of heat and inactivity? We were all of us there together, and yet we did not mesh our lives.

Dad was involved with the writing of his novel. He had submitted the first three chapters to his agent, who was now in the process of bargaining with a publisher, and Dad was hurriedly trying to finish a total outline before going to New York to work out the details of a contract.

As for Lisette, she always seemed to be busy doing something — dusting furniture, doing needlework, preparing meals. Sometimes she sat at the piano in the parlor and tinkled out delicate melodies that I had never heard before. On other occasions, she would change pace abruptly and start pounding out good, strong Dixieland that shook the walls. She spent a lot of time doing things with flowers and would spend long periods of time standing at the kitchen counter, arranging roses in antique vases and floating cream-colored gardenias in low, silver bowls.

Once or twice a week, Lisette drove into town to do errands and to shop for groceries. Often, on those occasions, Josie and I went with her to check books out of the library or take in an afternoon movie or simply to wander, browsing, through clothing shops and record stores.

Gabe did not, after my initial morning at Shadow Grove, express any further interest in accompanying us to Merveille. Instead, he seemed suddenly to have developed an all-consuming passion for fishing. Through a classified ad in the Sunday paper, he bought himself a secondhand rowboat with an outboard motor and moored it in the rushes across the road from us. From then on, we hardly saw him. Every morning, he would disappear with a fuel can and his fishing gear immediately after breakfast and would reappear around dinnertime, sometimes bringing back a few bass, but, more often than not, empty-handed.

Once, Lisette surprised me by suggesting that he take me with him.

"Don't you think that it's time that you showed Nore some of the scenery along the river?" she asked him. "It's like a whole foreign world back there, so green and lovely. I'm sure she's never seen anything quite like it."

Gabe shot his mother a quick, dark glance and shook his head.

"Not yet," he said. "There's plenty of time for that. We've got all summer."

"Sometimes it's better not to put things off too long," said Lisette. "You never know what problems may arise if you do."

"I said, *later*," Gabe told her brusquely. "I'm just not ready yet."

He turned on his heel and stalked angrily out of the room.

That evening, he didn't come home until after dark. The rest of us had long since finished eating, and Josie and I were out in the kitchen in the process of loading the dishwasher. Gabe entered the room without a word of greeting, served himself from the soup pot on the back of the stove, and left again, still without speaking. A moment later, I heard the sound of his feet crashing hard upon the stairs and realized that he was taking his supper up to his room.

"Why is he acting this way?" I asked Josie, not attempting to conceal my hurt and bewilderment. "He seemed to like me well enough when I first got here. When have I done to make him so angry now?"

"You haven't done anything," said Josie. "Gabe gets like this when he's under a lot of pressure. He's got things on his mind, that's all."

"What sort of things?" I asked her, and then — as a possible explanation occurred to me — "Could it be that girl he used to go with, the one who gave him the herbs he uses in the anisette? He said that she lived in a cottage over by the river. Do you suppose he might be seeing her again?"

"No," Josie said with certainty. "Felicité is gone. She and Gabe broke up a long time ago."

"Maybe she's changed her mind and come back," I suggested. If that were the case, it would explain so many things — the long hours Gabe spent away from home each day, the often nonexistent catch after a whole day's fishing, his resistance to his mother's request that he take me with him on one of his excursions on the river.

"That's impossible," said Josie. "Felicité's dead."

"Dead!" For some reason, I reacted with as much shock to that statement as if I had known Gabe's former girlfriend personally. "When did that happen? Did Gabe just find out about it? No wonder he's been acting so distant and preoccupied."

"It didn't just happen. Gabe's known about it for years," Josie said. "He wasn't all that upset by it, even back when it happened. By then, the two of them had been broken up for ages."

"He *wasn't upset by it!*" I repeated incredulously. "But, Jo, he *had* to be! Maybe they weren't still going together, but to have somebody your own age, someone you'd once really cared about, *die* —"

"It happens all the time, Nore," Josie said calmly. "Friends grow away from you, and they *do* die. That's why it's better not to get too attached to people. When you do, all that happens is that you end up sad."

Lying in bed that night, I thought back upon that statement and could hardly believe that the child had actually made it.

Despite her peculiarities, however, as the weeks slid past, I found myself developing a real fondness for my stepsister. With my father and Gabe so involved with their own activities, a lot of my time that summer was spent with Josie. I grew familiar with all her favorite records, and she, with the contents of my tape collection. We experimented with my blow dryer and curling iron, giving each other wild and wonderful hairdos; we took long walks along the bank of the river; and we lay in the sun, developing our tans, while a crew from a company called Holiday Pools, Inc., lined an oval-shaped pit with cement to create a swimming pool.

Often, in the late afternoons, when shade fell into the courtyard, we sat out behind the house in deck chairs and drank iced tea and played card games.

On one such occasion, Josie had just spread her winning hand out on the table and shouted, "Gin!" when a familiar voice spoke up unexpectedly from behind us.

"Aren't you a little young to be ordering cocktails, Miss?"

"Dave!" I exclaimed, turning in surprise. "Where did you materialize from, all of a sudden?"

"I didn't plan to burst in on you like this," Dave Parlange said apologetically. "I did ring the doorbell, but I guess you can't hear it out here. Celina said that your dad was working and Josie's mom was napping, but she thought I'd find the two of you around back."

"I'm so glad you're here!" Josie crowed happily, bouncing up from her chair like an excited puppy. "I've been wondering and wondering if you were really going to come!"

"How do you know Celina?" I asked, surprised by Dave's use of her name. "Did you meet her when you were out here doing the roofing?"

"All the old-time residents of Merveille know each other," Dave said. "It's like belonging to a club that goes back a hundred years. Celina was one year ahead of me in high school. Did you know that her grandfather, Charlie, used to work here as a gardener?"

"Did he really?" exclaimed Josie. "Maman will be interested to learn that. How long ago was it?"

"Way back before either you or your mother was born,"

said Dave. "I believe he said it was back in the nineteen-thirties. I ran into the old guy at the hardware store the other day. He was laughing about what a coincidence it is that another generation of his family should be working out at Shadow Grove for the Bergés."

"There's something sort of nice about that," I said. "It's like finishing a book and then suddenly finding there's a sequel. Sit down and cool off, Dave. Would you like some iced tea? I'd invite you to swim, but our pool doesn't have any water in it."

"That's no problem," said Dave. "I love to swim in dry pools; there's so little chance of drowning. No — seriously — I couldn't stay that long anyway. I've got to be leaving in just a few minutes. It's my sister's fourteenth birthday, and I've got to get her a present."

"Why did you go to the trouble of driving all the way out here, if you're just going to turn right around and go straight back?" In her usual, quicksilver manner, Josie had, in one instant's time, switched from a beaming smile to a petulant pout.

"I wanted to check with Nore about her plans for the weekend," said Dave. "Since you don't have a phone, this was the only way I could reach her."

It took a moment for the significance of the statement to register with Josie. When it did, the light drained abruptly from her face.

"You're asking *Nore* for a *date?*" she asked in a small, stunned voice.

"I thought we might take in a movie or something," Dave said. He plowed right ahead, oblivious to her reaction. "What do you say, Nore? Would you like to go out somewhere next Friday night?"

"I don't know," I said slowly. "It would be fun — but —"

My eyes shifted to Josie. The pain on her face was more than I could contend with. "It would be fun," I repeated, "but I can't. I'm sorry. I already have plans for Friday."

"Then, what about Saturday?"

"I'm busy on Saturday, too." I longed to cushion the refusal by offering some sort of explanation. I was afraid, though, that if I did, Dave would compound the problem by inviting me to go out with him the following weekend.

"I'm really sorry," I said lamely. "Thanks, though, for asking me."

"Yeah — well — those are the breaks, I guess."

I could tell that I had hurt him, but I could think of no way to soften the harshness of the rejection.

"Are you sure you don't want some iced tea?" I asked him awkwardly. "It's only about four right now. You don't have to leave quite yet. The stores in Merveille will be open for another few hours."

"No, thanks. Like I said, I've got to be heading back." His smile was a little too brilliant, the show of casualness a bit too elaborate, to be convincing. "Well, see you around, girls. Maybe we'll run into each other at the disco again."

"I hope so," I said. "I really do hope so, Dave."

There was nothing left to say then except "Goodbye." We both said that at once, avoiding each other's eyes in mutual embarrassment, and Dave left us the way he had come, disappearing around the corner of the house in several long-legged strides. A few minutes later, we heard the sound of his car starting up in the driveway. The roar of the engine seemed so loud in the afternoon stillness that I could not imagine how we could have missed hearing him arrive.

For long moments after his departure, Josie and I sat in silence.

It was I who finally broke it.

93

"Do you want to play another hand?" I asked.

"No." Josie had been staring down at the cards, spread face-up on the table between us. Now, she lifted her eyes to meet mine square on. "Why did you tell him that you were busy this weekend? You know that's a lie. All we're going to do is just sit around."

"I didn't come here to spend my summer dating," I told her. "I came here to be with my father and get to know my new family."

"That's not why you turned Dave down," Josie said. "You did it because of me. You knew that I wanted to go out with him, so you wouldn't." The expressive dark eyes — so much like Gabe's, so exactly like her mother's — were suspiciously bright. "That was nice of you, Nore, but you didn't have to do it. Gabe was right in what he said the other night. Nothing is ever going to work the way I want it to. No matter what I do — or what you do — or what anybody else does — nobody is ever going to fall in love with me."

"That's ridiculous!" I exclaimed. "You're only thirteen, Jo! When I was your age, I wasn't dating either!"

"But, then, you got to be fourteen — and fifteen — and sixteen!" Her voice was sharp with sudden, startling anger. "Guys like Dave think you're pretty. They won't even *look* at *me!*"

"In another few years —" I began.

"That won't make any difference!" The words were accompanied by a strangled sob. "I'm skinny — and I've got zits — and I don't have any boobs — and I'm ugly — ugly — ugly — ugly — ugly!"

The tears that she had been struggling so valiantly to hold back burst free in one great rush, as though a dam were breaking and a century's worth of pain were being spewed

94

forth. Instinctively, I opened my arms and held them out to her, and, just as instinctively, Josie jumped up to throw herself into them. Gathering the weeping youngster tightly against me, I rocked her back and forth as though I were her mother, shocked and bewildered by the intensity of the outburst.

"You are *not* ugly," I told her. "You're at a terrible age — thirteen. Boy, do I remember how awful it was! You're not a child any longer, and you've got all these strange, new feelings, but you're not an adult either, so there's nothing yet for you to do with them. What you've got to realize, Josie, is that everybody goes through this. In only a couple of years it will all be different."

"No, it won't!" Josie cried miserably. "Nothing's ever going to change, Nore! Time keeps going by, but it just doesn't count for anything!"

"It *does* count!" I said helplessly. "You just have to be patient. When you grow up, you're going to be beautiful!"

"No, I won't." The words were muffled by the pressure of her face against my shoulder. "I'm never going to look any different from what I do now."

"You will be *beautiful!*" I repeated with total sincerity. "How could you be anything else? Why, just look at your mother!"

"I *have* looked at Maman!" said Josie with frightening bitterness. "I look at her all the time, and I hate how she looks! I hate how she talks — how she acts — I hate everything about her!"

"You don't mean that," I said. "Oh, Josie, you know you don't mean that!"

But, even as I spoke, I knew keep in my heart that she did.

CHAPTER

10

It had been planned that I was to die on the following day. I was not aware of this, of course, as I lay on my bed the morning after Dave's visit to Shadow Grove, watching dawn break beyond the open doors to the balcony. Fire spilled into a crystal sky, and the gold rose slowly behind it, and then the blue. I thought about Josie and wondered if she was watching it also, lying in her own bed in the room next door to mine.

Josie had not been with us for dinner the previous evening. She had developed a headache after her tirade of weeping and had·gone upstairs to her room. It had fallen to me to explain the situation to Lisette, who had seemed more concerned about the fact that Dave had been to see us than about Josie's emotional reaction to his visit.

"What was he doing here?" she asked me. "The roofing was completed weeks ago. Why would one of the workmen come here now?"

"He wasn't just 'one of the workman,' " I said hesitantly. "He had gotten to be a — sort of — personal friend."

"A friend of whom?" asked Lisette. "Not of Gabe, I'm certain. You, yourself, only saw the young man once that I'm aware of, that time I asked you to go out and fetch Josie in for lunch. So, whom did he come here to see? What business did he have here?"

The truth of the matter — that we had all of us become more than casual acquaintances during an evening spent together at the disco — was impossible for me to offer. I glanced nervously across at Gabe in hopes that he would come up with something, but he was staring down into his plate as if he weren't following the conversation.

"I think this is something I'd better discuss with Josie," Lisette said finally, when neither Gabe nor I spoke up to volunteer an answer. "That girl has become so boy-crazy, she invites all kinds of liberties. I'm afraid that someday she may get herself into serious trouble."

True to her word, when dinner was over, she did go upstairs, and she remained in Josie's room for the rest of the evening. When I went up to bed at ten forty-five, I could hear the murmur of their voices, still rising and falling in serious discussion behind Josie's closed door.

I did not go directly to sleep that night. Instead, I lay awake for over an hour, staring out through the two French doors into the star-filled sky and thinking back upon the scene that had occurred that afternoon. No matter how hard I tried to sort things through, I continued to have the feeling that there had been something there that I had not been able to grasp. The weeping girl whom I had held in my arms had seemed, on the surface, to be as typical a thirteen-year-old as one could find, a reincarnation of myself at that miserable age, racked with all the insecurities common to early adoles-

97

cence. Yet, there had been some underlying current that I could not quite fathom — an intensity of feeling, a depth of pain, a strange sort of empty hopelessness — that I had never experienced at Josie's age, or, for that matter, *ever*.

Time passed, and eventually I did doze off, slipping from wakefulness into slumber in such minute gradations that I can pinpoint no true crossover point at which reality can be said to have given way to dreaming. As though sound had been put into slow motion, the voices in the adjoining room grew gradually louder, and the words of the conversation began to become clear to me. Although I knew at some level of fading consciousness that this could not actually be happening, it was as if I were standing, once again, at Josie's door with my ear to a drinking glass.

"If a romance should develop" . . . "You got us into this! You made the deal!" . . . "At Shadow Grove, I'm the one who is in control of things!" . . . "We can't go on like this, Maman!" . . . "Nore Robbins is a danger . . . a stranger . . . a danger . . ."

". . . in danger." Another voice rose, like an echo of Lisette's. "You and your father are both in terrible danger!"

I thought, but could not be certain, that the voice was my mother's.

At some point during that long and restless night, my dreaming must have been shaped and structured by the sound of the door to Josie's room opening and closing. In my dream state, I got up from my bed and slipped, ghost-like, through the wall, to trail my stepmother down the hall to the room she shared with my father. To my surprise, she did not enter, but continued on to the far west end of the hallway, where she opened the door to Gabe's room, stepped inside, and closed the door behind her.

Once again, I heard voices, low pitched but clearly distinguishable. "I said later ... I'm just not ready yet." ... "Sometimes it's better not to put things off too long." ... "We've got all summer." ... "Nore Robbins has an uncanny awareness of time!"

Then, suddenly, the whole scene changed, as though the channels on a television set had been abruptly switched and a new program was being shown. In this new vignette, I was standing on the bank of the river, but I was not alone there. I was in the midst of a group of people clothed in long, black robes, and every one of them was holding a candle. From behind us in the darkness there came the heavy, rhythmic beat of jungle drums, and at the river's edge, several yards away, there knelt five figures, one in a scarlet robe and the other four clothed in white.

"Watch, Nore! Please, watch carefully, Nore, and remember!"

I turned to see that my mother was standing beside me. Her normally smiling face was creased with worry, and her eyes were turned toward the little group by the river.

I followed her gaze and saw to my surprise that the figure in scarlet was not a man, but a woman. She appeared to be combining ingredients of some sort of an earthen bowl, and her four companions were watching the procedure with intense interest. After what seemed an eternity, the red-clad figure lifted the bowl in both hands and raised it high above her head. Swaying back and forth to the drumbeat, she began to chant. The words held no meaning for me, but the voice, low and guttural like the growl of a predatory animal, made my flesh crawl. The candle-bearers took up the chant, growling the strange, foreign syllables rather than speaking them, as the woman in scarlet lowered the bowl and bent to hold it in turn to the lips of each of the white-clothed figures kneeling at her feet. Then she threw back her head and uttered a long, shrill cry, and, blessedly, the vision vanished.

I must have tossed and turned incessantly during those dream sequences, for when I awoke the following morning I felt as exhausted as though I had really lived through all these experiences. Although I came awake at my usual early hour, I did not get up immediately to take my walk. Instead, I continued to lie there, watching the sunrise fade from the sky and listening to the chorus of bird voices twittering in the oak trees, until, without my planning to, I allowed my eyes to drop closed again. When I opened them for the second time an hour and a half later, the room was flooded with the brilliant light of full-blown morning.

It was the latest I had slept since my arrival at Shadow Grove. Although I knew in my rational mind that it was ridiculous to let one instance of oversleeping make me feel guilty, it was so ingrained in me to run on a regular schedule that I threw on my clothes in a rush that was almost panicky in a frantic effort to redeem myself.

As I descended the stairs, the smell of coffee rose to meet me, and I wondered if the rest of the family might still be at breakfast. This hope was squelched, however, when I passed through the downstairs hallway and heard the sound of my father's typewriter already clattering away behind the closed door to the study.

When I reached the kitchen, its sole occupant was Lisette. She was standing at the counter, slicing up the leftover ham from the previous night's dinner. Seen in silhouette against the window behind her, her facial features seemed almost unreal in their perfection. The knife she was holding made a firm, sharp clicking sound as it repeatedly descended upon the cutting board, sending slices of pink meat falling, one on top of another, in a neatly stacked pile.

"Well, hi there!" she said when she looked up to see me in the doorway. "What happened to that built-in alarm clock that we're all so in awe of? Did you forget to set it last night?

"Oh, I set it all right," I said sheepishly. "It went off at its usual time, but I guess I must have pushed my mental 'off' button. Why in the world are you making sandwiches at this hour? Or am I really so late that it's almost lunchtime?"

"You, with your time sense, must know better than that," said Lisette. "What I'm doing is fixing a picnic for you and Gabe to take with you out on the river."

"What do you mean, 'out on the river'?" I asked in bewilderment. "I thought that Gabe didn't want any company on his fishing trips."

"That was yesterday and the week before that," said Lisette. "That boy's changing moods are almost a match for his sister's. Out of the blue, he announced this morning that he's finally decided to introduce you to the bayou country. He asked me to tell you to come over to the boat when you've finished breakfast."

"All I want is coffee," I said, puzzled by this sudden turn of events. "Is Josie going with us? Is she waiting at the river, too?"

"Josie's still in her room," said Lisette. "You weren't the only one to sleep late this morning. Actually, I have to take responsibility for Josie. I was afraid that she'd never be able to settle down last night, so I gave her a pill to help her get to sleep."

"She *was* upset," I acknowledged, pouring coffee into a

mug. "She was crying so hard yesterday that it was almost scary."

"Jo is a high-strung girl," agreed Lisette. "Her adolescent hysteria gets totally out of hand. She has to realize that this Parlange boy is far too old to be interested in her. Obviously, the person he came here to see was Celina."

"Celina?" I exclaimed in surprise. "Why do you say that?"

"Josie told me that he and Celina went to high school together," said Lisette. "A lot of men seem to be attracted to Cajun women. Personally, I've always thought them to be rather coarse looking."

I was startled by the bitterness in her voice.

"I think Celina's quite pretty," I ventured tentatively.

"And quite promiscuous, too, I'll warrant," snapped Lisette. She seemed to assert a major effort to get a grip on herself. "Please, forgive me for that outburst, Nore. It must have sounded strange to you. I was being unfair, of course. Celina does seem to be a nice enough young woman, and I didn't have any right to imply that she wasn't. I have to keep reminding myself that this current generation should not be held responsible for the deeds of its ancestors."

"Speaking of ancestors, did you know that Celina's grandfather used to work at Shadow Grove?" I asked, seizing gratefully upon this chance to change the subject. "Back in the nineteen thirties, he was a gardener here."

"So Josie told me last night," said Lisette. "It's an odd coincidence, isn't it? I can only assume he was employed by my first husband's grandparents."

Our conversation lapsed into less threatening chitchat, and I sat down at the breakfast table to drink my coffee. As I sipped at the hot, black brew, Lisette continued to prepare the lunch for Gabe and me, placing the slices of meat be-

102

tween thick wedges of buttered French bread and wrapping the sandwiches in Saran Wrap. She placed those and some cookies and two cans of root beer in a small wicker picnic basket and set it on the table in front of me.

"There you are," she said. "I hope it's enough for the two of you."

"I'm sure it will be," I said, setting down my mug and getting to my feet. "Thanks so much, Lisette." I paused, and then continued, a bit awkwardly, "Thank you, too, for all the other nice things you've done for me. I really appreciate the way you've made me feel so welcome here."

There was a moment's silence.

Then, Lisette said quietly, "You're a nice girl, Nore. Josie told me about how kind you were to her yesterday. She said that she wished that the two of you were blood sisters. I, too, wish that your relationship with us were different."

Suddenly, to my surprise, she leaned forward and kissed me. "Run along now, dear. Have fun on your excursion with Gabe. My son is very fond of you. A mother can sense such things. It would have been wonderful if you and he could have met under other circumstances."

I left the house by the front door, and as I descended the porch steps, perfumed air rolled up to engulf me like a tidal wave. Honeysuckle and magolias poured forth their respective fragrances, and the mingled scents of the various flower-laden bushes that bordered the porch had already thickened in the heat of morning to a cloying sweetness. The long driveway lay stretched ahead of me like the dim aisle of a great cathedral, spotted with pagan coins of light that slipped through gold-paned windows. As I walked down to the gate beneath the canopy of oak leaves, I felt dwarfed by the immensity of the trees on either side of me.

At the driveway's end, I paused for a moment to brace myself for that initial step from the pleasant shade of the trees out into the full intensity of the blazing sunlight. When I did take that plunge, heat came pouring down upon me like molten copper, and within minutes my blouse was damp with perspiration and plastered to my back like a second skin. I hurried across the road, painfully aware of the heat that was rising in waves from the asphalt to attack my feet through the thin rubber soles of my sandals.

At this particular spot only a matter of several yards separated the shoulder of the road from the bank of the river. I saw Gabe immediately, standing at the water's edge with his back toward me. His shoulders were slumped, and he was leaning in a dejected manner against the bow of the weathered rowboat, which had been pulled up a foot or so onto solid ground. He was obviously listening for me, because he turned immediately when I stepped from the asphalt into the rustling grasses and stood, watching me walk toward him, with an expression on his face that was not likely to have made anybody feel very welcome.

"So, you did decide to come fishing today," he said. "I thought that maybe you wouldn't want to, all things considered."

"Your mother fixed us a lunch," I said, holding up the basket. "I thought that was a really nice thing for her to do."

"Sandwiches and cookies and stuff," Gabe said caustically. "That's a nice little touch, all right. Trust good old Maman to think of it." He gestured toward the boat. "Well, climb aboard if you're going to. I need you to weight down the stern so I can get us shoved off."

"I'm going to track in mud," I warned him, glancing down at my sandals which were already deeply embedded in the marshy earth.

"That doesn't matter," Gabe said. "Not with this old bucket. Go ahead — get in."

I did as directed, scrambling awkwardly over the side of the boat and almost dropping the picnic basket in the process. Once safely in, I set the basket on the floor by the center seat and moved to the back to add ballast to the end with the motor. Gabe threw himself against the bow, and there was an unpleasant, slurping sound as the boat began to slide backward across the wet mud and then settled into the river. Walking it out from the shore until he was knee-deep in water, Gabe grabbed hold of the side of the boat with both hands and hauled himself up and in.

The skiff lurched dangerously beneath the sudden new input of weight, and I clutched at the rusty engine for support.

"Be careful!" I exclaimed. "You almost tipped us over!"

"Sorry," Gabe said. "Look, Nore, I know that you're not much into water stuff. If this tipsy boat makes you nervous, why don't you just say so? Go on back to the house and tell Maman that you've changed your mind. There's nothing she can do about it if you decide that you don't want to come with me."

Actually, I had been contemplating doing exactly that. I was not pleased, however, to have Gabe be the one to suggest it.

"What are you trying to do," I asked, "get rid of me?" I was swept by a surge of perversity. "That's not going to be all that easy. You invited me to come today, so I'm afraid you're stuck with me. Where do you want me to sit?"

Gabe was silent for a moment. Then, with a shrug of defeat, he seemed to accept my decision as irrevocable.

"You can ride up in the front," he said. "It'll give us better balance."

105

He moved aside to let me edge past him. The boat kept dipping back and forth as I gingerly worked my way forward, and by the time I was settled on the small, triangular seat in the bow, we had drifted back to bob against the shore.

Gabe picked up an oar and pushed us away again. Then he seized the cord to the engine and gave it a vicious pull. The motor sprang into life with a sputtering roar. Gabe adjusted the throttle, and we began to chug out into the middle of the river.

It wasn't until we were a good hundred yards downstream that it occurred to me to wonder why the boat contained no fishing gear.

"W HERE are the poles and things?" I asked. "Wasn't this supposed to be a fishing trip?"

Gabe glanced down at the floor of the boat, as if expecting to see the poles materialize there.

"I must have forgotten to bring them," he said.

"Do you want to go back for them?" I asked him.

"Maybe in a little while," Gabe said. "For now, though, let's just concentrate on giving you a tourist's-eye view of the bayou country."

In perfect agreement with that suggestion, I turned my attention to the foreign scenery that now surrounded us. Within the few short minutes that we had been out upon the water, the river had routed itself far enough away from the highway so that we had put all signs of civilization behind us. The terrain that now enclosed us was a ghostlike forest of palmetto shrubs and live oak trees, the moss-draped branches of which hung above us like shabby, gray tents.

Knobby-kneed cypress rose from the river on either side of us, and the smooth, dark surface of the water threw back their reflections as perfectly as a mirror.

As we continued our slow-paced journey up the river, pale lavender flowers, which Gabe informed me were called water hyacinths, began to appear along side of our boat. The farther we went, the more numerous these blossoms became, until, eventually, they massed together to form one solid sheet of purple, which covered the surface of the river from one bank to the other. White herons, evidently disturbed by the noise of our motor, rose with screams of protest from the reeds at the water's edge and went streaking off into the treetops, dragging their long, strange legs behind them like excess baggage.

After we had traveled several miles of this world of shadows, the river suddenly widened, and the branches above us parted to let the sky show through. In this broader expanse of water, dead trees floated like lumpy corpses, caught in the tangle of roots from the clotted water-flowers. When I observed these logs more closely, I was surprised to discover that the "lumps" were not, as I had at first imagined, knots in the wood, but were turtles, lined up like cookies in the oven to soak up the sun.

Gabe idled the engine and then let it die completely. The silence that followed was like nothing I had never experienced. It was so deep and so intense that it seemed to contain some mysterious sound of its own, pitched at a level either too high or too low for human ears to decipher. Against this massive silence, the tiniest sounds were as startling as gunshots. The splash of a fish. The cry of a bird. The rustle of a squirrel, leaping from one tree limb to another.

"I see now why you like to come here," I said softly to

Gabe. "It's a whole different sort of world from the one we live in."

"It's a place where time doesn't seem to exist," said Gabe. "The outside world keeps changing, but back here everything stays the same."

"Josie made that same sort of statement yesterday," I told him. "She said her *life* is like that, locked in place with nothing ever changing."

"Poor Jo," Gabe said with sympathy in his voice. "I do believe life is harder for her than for any of us."

"It was strange," I said, "to hear that sort of statement from a thirteen-year-old. Do you have any idea what she could have been talking about?"

"There's not much about Josie that I don't know by this time," Gabe said. "My sister and I have known each other for a lot of years." Abruptly, he changed the subject. "There's a question I need to ask you, Nore." He paused, obviously searching for exactly the right words. "What would you say — to the idea — of our going away together?"

"Going away together!" I repeated in bewilderment, unable to believe that I had heard him correctly. "What do you mean? How could we do *that?*"

"We could take the Monte Carlo," Gabe said carefully. "Don't worry — you can do the driving — at least, until I work something out about getting myself a license. We could go back to the house right now, and you could wait for me out by the road while I slip into Maman's room to get her keys. Then we could just take off."

"Take off to go *where?*" I asked him.

"Anywhere we want. California might be a good place to start. There are a lot of young people out there on the Coast, all coming and going; nobody ever knows exactly who anybody is. We could rent an apartment and maybe get jobs as movie extras. Or you could waitress, and I could work down on the docks or something. It wouldn't much matter, as long as we were free and together."

"You want us to *live together?*" I whispered incredulously. "But you're not even in love with me!"

"I could be," Gabe said, "if I let myself. How about you? Do you think you could fall in love with me if you tried?"

"I — might," I said hesitantly, reluctant to admit that I had been half in love with him ever since my first day at Shadow Grove. "I don't understand, though — if you feel this way about me, why have you been acting the way you have? You've hardly even spoken to me since that night at the disco."

"It hit me, that night, how hopeless the whole thing was," said Gabe. "I didn't want to get any more attached to you than I had to. I didn't think there was any chance of things working out for us, and it's so damned hard when you care about people and then have to — lose them. Then I got this idea about our going away together. It could be the answer, Nore — at least for four or five years. Are you willing to give it a try?"

"Why do we need to run off like criminals to be together?" I asked him. "We live in the same house right *now*. Why can't we wait, at least until we graduate from high school? That would give us some time to find out if we were really right for each other."

"That's impossible," said Gabe. "It has to be now, or it's never."

"Why?" I regarded him blankly. "I don't understand."

"Of course you don't. You'll just have to take it on faith

that I know what I'm talking about. Félicité didn't understand either — at least, not at first."

"Félicité? You mean, your old girlfriend?"

"She wasn't just a girlfriend," Gabe told me. "She and I lived together like husband and wife for almost eight years."

"You couldn't have done that!" I exclaimed. "You're just seventeen *now!* When did this big romance take place — when you were nine years old?"

"I know you won't be able to accept this, but we were both seventeen when Félicité and I fell in love," Gabe said. "Eight years later, she was more of a mother to me than a sweetheart. An older man came along, and that was the end of our relationship. They got married, and I went back to live at Shadow Grove."

"What you're saying makes no sense at all," I said irritably. "I hate it when you play games with me this way. This was the way you were talking that night on the way back from the disco. It isn't funny, Gabe; it's just terribly upsetting."

"Then, you won't go," Gabe said. It was a statement, rather than a question.

"No, of course I won't go," I told him. "It's a crazy idea. I'd never hurt my father that way; he'd worry himself sick about me. Besides, it just wouldn't work. We'd never be able to support ourselves. Kids our age aren't ready for that kind of live-together setup."

There was a long moment of silence, broken only by a splash as one of the turtles slid off its log and sank into the river. It went down like a stone, and from the spot at which it had entered the water, ripples moved out in a series of ever-widening circles.

Then, Gabe said with stolid acceptance, "All right. That's it, I guess."

He reached down and took hold of the rope that activated the engine. His jaw was set, and his eyes would not meet mine.

"Don't be angry," I said more gently, regretting my use of the hurtful term *crazy*. The romantic idea had not been crazy, just totally unworkable. "This doesn't mean that everything's over, Gabe. We have so much time —"

"It *does* mean that everything's over," Gabe said quietly. "I'm not angry, Nore, I'm just sorry — just terribly sorry."

He gave the rope a sharp yank, and the engine caught immediately. Gabe set it on idle, and then, at last, turned to look at me. There was pain in his eyes, but, when he spoke, his voice was expressionless.

"How about getting out some sandwiches before we head back? I know it's early for lunch, but I didn't get much breakfast."

"Neither did I," I said, relieved at the change of subject. "Don't start up the boat yet. I'll get the picnic basket."

Getting up from my seat in the bow, I moved cautiously back toward the center of the skiff, taking care not to set it to rocking with any sudden movement. Bending down carefully, I picked up the basket from the floor by the middle seat and stood, balancing myself, while I unhooked the latch that held the lid in place.

"Your mother made ham —" I began.

At that moment, the engine came to life with a mighty roar and the boat shot forward. An instant later, the peace of the swampland was shattered by a jarring crash, and I felt myself being catapulted backward over the bow of the boat, still clutching the picnic basket, too shocked even to scream. The last thing I remember seeing before I struck the water was a wide arch of blue, filled suddenly with thrashing wings, as water birds rose from the marshes on every side of us and exploded in one wild burst into the shelter of the sky.

The river closed around me, and I went down, weighted by clothing and terror, plunging like the turtle into the thick, soupy water until I actually felt my face brush the river floor. For one frantic moment, the thought occurred to me that I might be destined to stay there forever, sucked in and immeshed and swallowed, coated with stickiness, caught by the mud like a fly in a jar of honey.

Almost immediately, however, I felt myself beginning to rise again. At some point during my descent, I had released my grip on the basket, and now, with my hands unencumbered, I raked wildly at the water in a feverish attempt to claw my way with my bare fingernails up out of the brown depths of the river into the world of light.

I was still clawing, when my hands and then my head broke surface. Choking and strangling, I dragged in a great gasp of tepid air. When I blinked the water out of my eyes, I saw our boat, rocking peacefully back and forth like a cradle, only a few yards away. Gabe was seated in the stern in exactly the same position that he had been in before the accident. I could only imagine that his grip on the rudder control handle had prevented him from being sent flying out as I had.

"Gabe!" I tried to call out to him, "Gabe — I can't — I can't —"

He *knew* that I couldn't swim! I had told him that on my very first morning at Shadow Grove, when the two of us had stood chatting together down by the lily pond. Was it possible that he could have forgotten and actually be thinking that I was capable of swimming across to the boat?

"Gabe — please!" I gasped, and felt myself going under once more. This time, I descended more slowly, but with a sort of leaden certainty. My feet struck bottom and seemed to keep right on going, sinking into the gummy sediment as though they belonged there.

After what seemed like hours, I did begin to rise again, but this, too, happened slowly. My chest felt ready to burst by the time I again reached the surface of the water. My head thudded hard against something solid, and I reached up and grabbed it, shoving it out at arm's length in front of me so that I could come up behind it.

Clinging for dear life to whatever it was that I was grasping, I spat out a mouthful of water and hungrily sucked in air. When I had gained enough control of my senses to fully comprehend things, I saw that the object of my salvation was a floating log.

It was probably this that our boat had gone plowing into. But where had that boat disappeared to? I could see it nowhere. Clutching the log, I glanced wildly around me in all directions. When, at last, I did spot the skiff, I could not believe what I was seeing. It was a good fifty yards downriver, chugging rapidly along like a squat, gray pony headed determinedly for its stable. All that I could make out of Gabe was the back of his head. He did not even turn back to look over his shoulder.

I stared after the boy and the boat with increasing horror.

"Come back!" I tried to scream, but the sound that emerged from my throat was no more than a whimper. In another few moments, the boat was a speck in the distance. Then it disappeared altogether around a bend in the river.

Gabe had deliberately gone off and left me to drown!

The mere idea of his having done this was so incomprehensible that I could not immediately absorb it. For an unreasonably long time, I stayed where I was without moving, clinging to my makeshift life preserver and waiting hopefully for the skiff to reappear. It was not until the herons had begun to settle, lured back to their places of residence by the unbroken quiet, that I was able to accept the situation for what it was.

Gabe was *not* coming back. He had no intention of trying to save me. If I were going to survive this adventure, I was the one who would have to get myself back to dry land.

In my logical mind, I was no longer frightened of drowning. My log seemed remarkably buoyant, and as long as I kept my hold on it, there was little chance of my going under again. With this fear set on a back burner of my mind, I immediately turned my thoughts to other dangers, such as the sorts of creatures that might be sharing the river water with me. Alligators, water snakes, and leeches were almost as horrible to contemplate as drowning had been. I would have to get to shore, and the sooner the better.

By twisting my shoulders with quick, hard jerks, I was eventually able to work the log around so that it angled toward the south bank of the river. Then, using the water-swollen wood as a paddle board, I started an awkward flutter kick, which slowly moved me in the direction that I wanted to go.

As I drew closer to land, my progress was slowed even further by the masses of water hyacinths that blocked my way. These deceptively delicate-looking flowers, which had been sparsely scattered through the center of this wider portion of the river, became increasingly more numerous closer to the shoreline, and their long, trailing roots intertwined to form a net of snakelike coils. Tearing a pathway through this was far from easy, and I was as exhausted physically as I was emotionally by the time that I finally dragged myself out of the water.

I did not stop to rest, however. I was too filled with adrenaline — too hurt, too angry — too determined to get to my father and inform him of the incredible thing that had happened. Turning my left shoulder toward the sun, I set off toward the south, the direction in which I knew the highway must lie. My soaked sandals slurped across mud and caught on high grasses. I shoved my way through shoulder-high thickets of palmetto shrubs and thrust aside low-hanging tree limbs, and with every step I took, I grew more and more furious.

By the time that I had reached the road, my mind was centered upon one thing only — the fact that Gabe, who had just finished telling me that he wanted to live with and love me, had not only tried to kill me, but had come very close to succeeding.

CHAPTER

12

I arrived back at Shadow Grove at twenty past twelve. The fact that I managed to get there so quickly was thanks to a middle-aged woman in a gray Chrysler who stopped to offer me a ride. I had never accepted a ride from a stranger in my life before, but I did not hesitate a second before accepting this one. Even if she had turned out to be the Boston Strangler in disguise, there would have been nothing that I could have imagined her doing to me that would have begun to measure up to the experience that I had just been through.

Of course, she did nothing, except to spread newspapers out to protect her upholstery and to ask with concern what had happened to have caused me to get so wet. I was too worked up at this point to tell her anything but the truth, or, at least, a portion of it; I said that I had gone fishing with a friend and fallen out of the boat, and that the boy I was with had gone off and left me.

"A lovers' quarrel," the woman said knowingly. "Dump him, honey. No guy who would do a thing like that is worth a plug nickel."

"I'm going to dump him, all right," I told her vehemently, and to myself I added silently, "When Dad learns what happened today, he and I will be dumping this whole weird family."

The woman left me off in front of the gate to Shadow Grove, and I trudged up the long driveway, finding it hard to believe that a few short hours earlier I had come swinging down it, basket in hand, as happy and unsuspecting as Little Red Riding Hood on her classic, near-fatal trip to her grandmother's house.

The first person I saw when I entered the house was Lisette. As I stepped through the front doorway, I could see straight across the entrance hall into the parlor. My stepmother was seated there on the sofa, in a posture of waiting, and from the stunned expression that crossed her face when she saw me, it was evident that I was not the person she was expecting.

I did not speak or in any other way acknowledge Lisette's existence. Instead, I wheeled on my heel and continued down the hall to my father's study. When I reached it, I flung open the door and hurried in.

Dad turned from his typewriter, obviously startled by my abrupt and unannounced entrance. His eyes grew wide and alarmed as they took in my condition.

"Good Lord, Nore, what happened to you?" Dad exclaimed. "You look like a drowned kitten!"

"I almost became one," I said, my voice ringing out so shrill and strange that I hardly recognized it as being my own. "Gabe almost drowned me!"

"Gabe almost drowned you!" Dad repeated blankly. "What, in God's name, are you talking about?"

"Just what I said," I told him. "Gabe took me out for a boat ride on the river, and when I was standing up and not holding onto anything, he ran the boat full-speed into a log. I was thrown out into the water, and I almost drowned!"

"Good Lord!" Dad said again. "Thank God, you're all right! Where is Gabe? Is he okay too?"

"Of course!" I cried. "What could possibly happen to Gabe? He's some sort of magic man! He can squeeze a half-dozen lifetimes into seventeen years!"

And then, I did something that I have never fully forgiven myself for. I burst into tears.

If I had stood there and told him my story calmly and coherently, I believe that perhaps I might have convinced Dad to believe me. I lost that chance, however, the moment that I let myself start crying. Once begun, the tears would not stop; they just kept pouring out, and every measure of control I had went right down the drain.

Within seconds, I was sobbing so hard that I could not talk.

Dad jumped up from his chair and came over to put his arms around me.

"Nore, honey," he said gently. "Poor baby, you must have been terrified."

"Chuck!" Lisette's voice spoke from the doorway behind me. "What's happened? What's the matter with Nore? Is she hurt?"

"The kids had a little accident in Gabe's boat," Dad said. "Nore says they're both okay, but she fell in the river. She isn't a swimmer, so, of course, she was terribly frightened."

"Poor child!" exclaimed Lisette. "What an unfortunate

thing to have happen! I've told Gabe over and over that he ought to carry life preservers."

"You wouldn't normally expect to need them on such a narrow strip of water," Dad said. "Gabe undoubtedly didn't realize that Nore couldn't swim. Is there anything we can give her to calm her down a little? Some tea, maybe, or some brandy?" He tightened his arms around me. "Nore, baby, try to get a grip on yourself. You *are* okay. You *did* make it through. Gabe got you home safely."

"No, he didn't!" I tried to tell him, but the words never quite came out. The more that I struggled to speak, the more impossible it became.

Dad sat down in his desk chair and pulled me onto his lap, cradling me against him in the same way that he had when I was tiny and had awakened from a nightmare. It flashed into my mind that this was the same way that I had held and comforted Josie on the previous day. For some reason, the irony of that realization caused me to cry even harder. I had *cared* about Josie — I had cared about *all* of Dad's new family — never knowing, never guessing, that they were my *enemies!*

It was several minutes before I heard Lisette's voice again. When I did, it was close beside us.

"Here, Chuck, try this. It always seems to work for Josie."

"Thanks, Lis," Dad said. "Listen, Nore, I want you to drink this. Now, stop being foolish!" as I jerked backward and tried to push his hand away. "It's just anisette, and you only need to take a swallow. You've got to get over this hysteria, or you're going to make yourself sick."

He held the cordial glass to my mouth and shoved the rim between my lips. For one crazy moment, I envisioned myself shattering it with my teeth and spatting out a shower of bloody saliva and shards of glass. I knew, though, that this sort of resistance would not get me anywhere. There was not enough strength left in me to combat the combined forces of Lisette and my father.

With a feeling of utter helplessness, I parted my lips and allowed the sweet, dense syrup to be poured into my mouth. Even as I swallowed, I sensed that there was something in it that should not have been there. A few moments later, my suspicions were confirmed, as I felt the impact of the potion hit my stomach. A wave of dizziness struck me, and I clung more tightly to my father, pressing my face against the comforting bulk of his shoulder.

"There," Dad said gently, as my sobbing became less frenzied. "There, now — I told you this would make you feel better."

"It was poisoned," I whispered. "It's making me feel funny."

"It was anisette, Nore, and all it's doing is relaxing you." He rose from the chair, gathering me up in his arms as easily as though I were still a small child and it were my bedtime. "Let's get you upstairs, and Lisette can help you get changed. Then, you can lie down for a while and after you're feeling more rested —"

"No!" I protested weakly. "Not Lisette — you! You stay with me, Daddy! Don't leave me alone with Lisette!"

"All right, all right," Dad said soothingly. "Please, don't be offended, Lis. Nore isn't herself right now. She doesn't know what she's saying."

"I understand perfectly," said Lisette. "You go ahead and take care of your daughter, dear. I'm going across the road to see if I can find my son. As fond as Gabe is of Nore, he's sure to be terribly upset about what's happened. He may be feeling so guilty that he can't bring himself to come in and face us."

I don't remember very much about what happened after that. The world was spinning too wildly for me to fully take things in. I do know that Dad carried me up the stairs and into my bedroom, and I have some faint recollection of his opening the drawer and getting out dry clothes for me to put on. I know I kept trying to tell him things, but my words kept slurring together, and even to my own ears the results of my efforts were little more than gibberish.

"Don't leave me," I managed to mumble, "please, Dad, don't leave me!" I caught at his hand, and clung to it, as I had to that log in the river. "Don't leave —"

And then, sleep rolled in upon me in a thick, dark wave, and I was lost.

I slept for six straight hours, and when, at last, I awakened, I felt sick to my stomach and my mouth tasted stale and sour. The room was soft with twilight, and my father's hand no longer lay in mine.

When I turned my head on the pillow, however, I saw him seated in a chair not far from my bedside, making penciled notes on pages of manuscript. He had the look of a person who had been rooted to one spot for an extensive length of time.

"Daddy?" I said tentatively. My voice was cracked and hoarse, but understandable. I tried it again. "Daddy?"

"So, you've finally decided to join us in the land of the living," Dad said, looking up with a smile that was as weary as it was welcoming. He laid his papers aside and got up to come over to the bed. "I was starting to wonder if maybe I shouldn't wake you. When I suggested that you get some rest, I didn't expect you to make that a lifetime career."

"Have you been here all along?" I asked him.

"Most of the time," Dad said. "I went downstairs for a while when Lisette came back with Gabe. He was one relieved boy when he learned that you were safe."

"I just bet," I said sarcastically. "Where is he now, Dad? I want to see him. I want to talk with him, right here in front of you."

"I'm afraid that will have to wait," Dad told me quietly. "Lisette's driven Gabe in to Merveille to be checked at the hospital. She wants to be sure that he doesn't have a concussion."

"A concussion!" I exclaimed. "What do you mean by that? Nothing happened to Gabe. He wasn't even thrown in the water."

"That's true enough," Dad said, "but he *was* thrown off his seat. His head hit the side of the boat, and he was knocked unconscious."

"That's not true!" I protested. "Gabe wasn't hurt at all! After I hit the water and came back up again, I saw him sitting right there in the stern as though nothing had happened."

"You don't know what you're saying, honey," Dad said. "I saw Gabe's forehead. He has a lump there the size of a goose egg."

"Then he was the one who put it there," I said. "He must have hit himself with something, or maybe he rammed his head against a tree. Or perhaps he had his mother do it for him. If Lisette brought him back to the house, it means that she had some time alone with him while you were up here with me."

Dad regarded me incredulously. "How can you suggest such a thing! Why would Gabe deliberately injure himself?

And *Lisette?* You know how much Lisette loves her children. They mean the world to her. She would die before she would ever hurt either one of them."

"She'd do it if she had to in order to back up Gabe's story," I said. "That story's a lie, Dad. Gabe wasn't hurt, he just took off on me. He didn't try to save me when I fell into the water. Even worse than that, I feel sure he rammed that log on purpose."

"That's a terrible thing to say." All the former warmth was gone from my father's voice. "I know that you've been through a traumatic experience, Nore, and I appreciate how upset you are, but what you're suggesting is beyond anything I will consent to listen to. Accidents do happen, and while I'm not happy with Gabe for having been so careless, there's no way in the world that I'm willing to believe that he did this deliberately."

"Then, why did he go off and leave me?" I asked belligerently. "Why didn't he jump into the water and rescue me? He *knew* I couldn't swim, and yet, he just sat there. That final time when I came to the surface, that time I grabbed hold of the log, Gabe was way down the river, already headed for home."

"You were scared and disoriented," Dad said. "You're simply not remembering right."

"I may have been scared, but I remember everything I saw!" I sat up on the bed. My head started spinning, but I held my upright position, gritting my teeth. "Where is Josie? Let's bring in Josie! I bet there are lots of things that she can tell us!"

"Lisette took Josie with her," Dad said. "Jo hasn't been well today. She slept straight through the morning and didn't wake up until after you had your accident. When she heard about what happened, she became so upset that Lisette didn't want to leave her."

"That figures," I said bitterly. "Of course Lisette got Jo out of here. She didn't want us pumping her while she was gone. I bet that Lisette doped her up last night, just the way she did me today, so that she'd be out of the picture this morning and couldn't interfere with things. She knew that Josie had gotten to like me, and she didn't want to run the risk of having her do something to spoil the plan."

"I don't like all this talk about 'doping people up,'" Dad said. "All Lis gave Josie last night was a very mild tranquilizer, and this afternoon you had a sip or two of anisette. I have a small glass of that with Lisette every night after dinner. It's never sedated me to any degree."

"It did once," I told him. "It was the second night I was here. Remember how you and Lisette both got sleepy so early? That was Gabe's doing. He poured your liqueurs from his own special 'sleepytime' stash. That liquor's been treated with herbs that a witch girl gave him. I bet this family's into all sorts of witchcraft stuff. Lord knows what kinds of things Lisette keeps in *her* medicine cabinet!"

"That's enough of that, Nore," my father said angrily. "I don't want to hear any more of this. I'm going to go downstairs now and fix some supper. I don't know how Gabe is going to be feeling when his mother gets him back here, but Lis and Josie will probably be needing some nourishment. After you've pulled yourself together, come down and join me. I warn you, though, I'm not going to listen to any rerun of these crazy accusations. These are my wife and stepchildren that you're talking about. I happen to care for them deeply, even if you don't."

The tone of his voice left no room for further argument.

Even if that had not been the case, there would have been nothing more that I could have told him. It was little wonder that my father refused to believe me. The statements that I had been making *did* sound crazy.

As soon as Dad was out of the room, I got up from the bed and headed for the bathroom. The dizziness that had overwhelmed me earlier had still not completely vanished. I felt shaky and nauseated, and my tongue was coated and sticky. I could hardly wait to rinse my mouth out and brush my teeth.

The face that looked back at me from the mirror over the washbasin was hardly recognizable as my own. It was pale and glassy-eyed, and my hair, which had been plastered wet against my skull and then slept on, was as matted as a doll's wig.

I got out my toothbrush and toothpaste and scrubbed my mouth out, and then got into the shower and turned the water on full blast. As I scrubbed the muck of the riverbed off my body, I pondered the most immediate problem that confronted me. I would somehow have to prove to Dad that my suspicions about my stepfamily were not all products of an overactive imagination. Without that, I would never be able to get him to leave Shadow Grove, which was something that I was convinced was an absolute necessity. My dream of my mother's warning had been prophetic; every moment we stayed on the premises we were in danger.

After the conversation that Dad and I had just had, it was evident to me that there was no way that I could get him to accept the fact that Gabe had tried to kill me. He had been too well conditioned by Gabe and Lisette during the time that I had been sleeping. What *might* be possible to prove, though, was that I had been drugged — that herbal potions were available at Shadow Grove — and that the Bergé family used them to suit their purposes. Although this was a far cry from proving attempted murder, I had the feeling that if I could force Dad to open the door of his mind a crack to the possibility that there were certain things about his new family that were not as they should be, that crack would enlarge on its own to permit entrance to other, more serious suspicions.

I, myself, was sure that the cordial that Lisette had given me that afternoon had contained a sedative. I could think of no way to prove this, though, without obtaining a sample of the concoction. That possibility seemed like a dead-end street. It was almost a certainty that the drug had been placed directly into my glass, rather than into the anisette bottle, and that glass would undoubtedly by now have been thoroughly rinsed out.

But I *did* have access to the "sleepytime" anisette that Gabe kept in his room. If I took a sample of that to a pharmacy in Merveille, they would be able to advise me about how to get it analyzed. My heart started beating faster as this idea began to take form. The whole Bergé family was out of the house now, which was an unusual occurrence. If there was ever to be an opportunity to get my hands on Gabe's supply of anisette, it was now.

Letting the comb in my hand drop unceremoniously into the sink, I left the bathroom and hurried down the hall to Gabe's room. To my relief, the door wasn't locked. I turned the knob, gave a hard shove, and stepped inside.

I don't know what exactly it was that I expected to find there — the den of a monster? an open coffin? a mummified corpse? I have to admit that my imagination had become obstreperous as a result of the events of the morning. What I *did* find was both a relief and a disappointment; it was the typical cluttered habitat of a teenage boy. The bed was unmade, and on the floor beside it, there lay an empty pop can and a pile of candy bar wrappers. Gabe's shorts and running shoes had been tossed into a corner, along with a dingy T-shirt and a pair of dirty socks. The shelf above the bed held a radio and tape player, a selection of books, and a partially constructed airplane model. One wall of the room was decorated with photographs of sports personalities, and a *Playboy* centerfold had been taped to another.

After giving the room as a whole a quick review, I turned my attention to the bureau. Nervously, I gripped the brass handles of the topmost drawer and pulled. The drawer slid easily outward, displaying such a jumbled assortment of clothing that it was obvious that Gabe was accustomed to putting away his own laundry. Plunging both hands into the drawer, I rummaged among the socks and underwear, groping about for some container that liquor might be stored in. The only bottle I found was one labeled "Brut," and, upon opening it, I discovered that it contained after-shave lotion.

Shoving that drawer closed, I performed the same investigation on the second drawer and then on the third. Each search met with the same lack of success. The final drawer did not contain a bottle either, but as I ran my hand along the bottom of it, my fingers came into contact with something that didn't seem to belong there. It felt at first like a flat piece of cardboard, but when I got a grip on one corner and lifted it out to inspect it, I found that it was a mounted photograph. Evidently the product of one of those novelty studios that specialize in period settings, it showed a family of five, posed formally together, dressed in old-fashioned costumes.

The seated woman and two of the children I recognized instantly as Lisette, Gabe, and Josie. A second teenage boy stood behind Lisette, with one hand on her shoulder. Although he bore a strong resemblance to Gabe, he was shorter and stockier, and his squared-off chin gave the impression of stubborn rebelliousness. The man in the picture could have been the children's great-grandfather. He was wrinkled and frail-looking, and sat in the slumped position often assumed by the feeble elderly.

As I stood, studying the photograph, I suddenly became aware of the sound of a car motor. Glancing out through the open louvers of the door to the balcony, I was startled to see Lisette's Monte Carlo turning in at the gate. As the car approached the house, it moved out of my line of vision, but in a few minutes I was aware of the fact that the engine had gone silent. Then, there was the sound of car doors opening and slamming, and the indistinct murmur of voices, one of them masculine.

They were home — Lisette and Josie — and Gabe must have come back with them. Despite his supposed injury, he must not have been hospitalized.

I knew that I had to get out of Gabe's room immediately. Giving the photograph one final glance, I started to thrust it back into the drawer.

Then I hesitated. Although I knew that I had never met him, there was something about the elderly man in the picture that was oddly familiar. His was a face that I was used to seeing somewhere else; in another form, perhaps, and in a different setting. The eyes — I knew those eyes — and the old-fashioned frock coat. Where in the world had I seen someone wearing *that?*

When the answer struck me, it did not make things much

clearer. It wasn't this man I was recalling, it was his *picture*. Although he was many years older in this photograph, it was he who was the subject of the oil painting that hung in the parlor.

Even as this thought occurred to me, I knew that I had to be wrong. The portrait downstairs was obviously a very old one. The man who had sat for it would be long deceased by now. There was no way that he could have posed with Lisette and her children for what, judging by their ages, had to have been a recent photograph.

There was no way that he could have — and yet — he *had*.

The moment that I accepted that proposition as fact was the moment that the whole world seemed to fall out from under me.

CHAPTER

‑‑•⊰ 13 ⊱•‑‑

I did not replace the photograph in Gabe's drawer. I carried it, instead, back to my own room and slid it into the narrow space between the headboard of my bed and the wall.

Not that it remained there for any extended period, for during the days that followed, I took it out often. I would lie on my bed for hours on end and study it, while in the blue sky beyond the open French doors, the strange, swirling clouds of a Louisiana summer writhed and wrinkled in heat and rising humidity that was becoming all but unbearable.

My closer inspection now revealed to me that I had been wrong in my assumption that the picture had been taken recently and that the people in it were wearing costumes. When I removed the photograph from its mount, I discovered that it had not been printed upon modern photographic paper but upon a silvery sheet of very thin metal and that the cardboard behind it was so browned and brittle with age that it crumbled in my hands.

Yet, the woman was Lisette, there was no doubt of that. And Gabe and Josie were simply Gabe and Josie — looking as they did now, except for their clothing and hairstyles. Josie was dressed in a long skirt and white gloves and was wearing a hat, but there was no mistaking the high cheekbones and the huge, dark eyes. Gabe wore an odd-style suit, and his hair was cut very short. The other boy in the picture was wearing knickers. That boy was not familiar to me, but I knew who he had to be. He was Lisette's second son, the one who had died many years ago. He was Louis.

Except for meals, during which my father was present, I tried to avoid all contact with the Bergés. This was not difficult to do, as they made no effort to press themselves on me. The pool was now completed and filled with water, and Josie spent most of her time either swimming in it or stretched out on a beach towel next to it, reading one of her romance novels. Lisette, although she was as pleasant to me as always, did not question the amount of time that I spent in my room alone or try to coax me to accompany her on shopping trips. It was as if a transparent wall had suddenly slipped between us, a wall that no one needed to acknowledge, but all except my father were aware of.

My only confrontation with Gabe occurred on that very first evening when he and Lisette and Josie returned from Merveille. After I had concealed the confiscated photograph in my room, I went downstairs to the kitchen where the whole family had now gathered. Although my father had heated up soup and made a salad, nobody seemed to be in any rush to eat. Josie's eyes were red and puffy as though she had been crying. Lisette was in the process of pouring herself a glass of sherry.

Gabe was slumped in a chair at the kitchen table. His face

was pale, and he did have a lump on his forehead, which looked painful and awful.

"Why did you do it?" I asked him in front of all of them. "Why did you go off and leave me to drown?"

Gabe raised his head and looked me straight in the eyes.

"I didn't do that," he said. "I was knocked unconscious. When I came to, there wasn't any sign of you anywhere — not in the boat — not in the water. I shouted your name, and I didn't get any answer. I didn't know what had happened to you. It was terrifying."

"That's not true," I said. "You weren't hurt — at least, not then. When I was thrashing in the water, I saw you in the boat. You weren't looking for me — you weren't calling — you weren't doing anything but sitting there. When I surfaced for the second time, you were way down the river."

"I don't know how you can say that, Nore," said Gabe.

"She was panicked," Dad said apologetically. "She was hallucinating. People's senses can play strange tricks under stress."

"I wasn't —" I tried to protest, and then let the sentence trail away as I saw the closed expression on my father's face. He had made it clear already that he did not believe me. To prolong the scene with Gabe was not going to accomplish anything except to cause even more estrangement between us.

I don't know that I have ever felt so helpless and as isolated as I did during the week that followed that incident on the river. The conjectures that were building within me were too horrendous to keep to myself, yet there was no one with whom I could share them. If Dad refused even to listen to my accusations about Gabe, I could imagine what his reaction would be if I were to confront him with the other suspicions that were beginning to form in my mind.

What I needed was someone to talk with who knew the Bergés. The more I thought about this, however, the more I had to realize that there were no such people. Lisette and her children had no social life of any kind. There were no neighbors within many miles of Shadow Grove. No mail ever arrived there, except for business correspondence addressed to my father. Since there was still no telephone, no one ever received any phone calls. It was as if this family had deliberately placed itself on a deserted island, totally out of reach of other human beings. The only outsiders who had set foot on the grounds since my arrival had been workmen hired to perform impersonal services, and Dave Parlange, who had paid me one short visit in order to invite me to the movies.

And, of course — Celina.

Celina!

As the thought of Lisette's cleaning girl flashed into my mind, my heart suddenly quickened. Although her personal experience in working at Shadow Grove was of short duration, Celina's family association with the place went back two generations. If Dave was correct about her grandfather's having worked there during the 1930s, then he was the one who might be able to provide me with the information I needed.

The next Tuesday night I was too excited to sleep. I lay awake for hours, making plans for the following day. I decided that the best procedure would be to intercept Celina before she ever got to the house and to ask her if she would give me her grandfather's phone number. The reason I would give for wanting this would be that I was helping my father do research for his new book and needed to ask some questions of a long-time resident of the area. Once I obtained the number, I would take the Pontiac and drive into town where I could get access to a telephone. If I acted quickly enough, I might be able to accomplish everything I needed to do before anyone in the family realized what was happening.

Celina's workday was scheduled to begin at eight-thirty. By eight, I was standing at the end of the driveway, waiting for her Volkswagen bug to come chugging up to the gate. One hour later, I was still standing there and still waiting. By nine-fifty, I finally had to acknowledge to myself that my plan was not going to work out as I had hoped it would. Bitterly disappointed, I returned to the house.

The first thing I was aware of as I entered was the sound of my father's voice in the parlor. When I looked in, I saw him, seated in one of the wing chairs, reading aloud from the most recent chapter of his manuscript. Lisette and Josie, a rapt audience, were seated on the sofa across from him.

"Where's Celina?" I asked, breaking in on the recitation. "This is Wednesday. Shouldn't she have gotten here by now?"

"Please, don't interrupt, Nore dear," Lisette said gently but firmly, as Dad paused in his reading. "Your father is sharing some very wonderful passages."

"I'm sure he is," I said shortly. "Everything he writes is wonderful. What I want to know is, where is Celina?"

"Celina won't be working here any longer," said Lisette.

"She won't!" I exclaimed. "Why not?"

"I've let her go," Lisette told me. "I wrote her a letter, giving her notice, last weekend. I enclosed a full month's wages, so the girl won't suffer any from the dismissal. With domestic help as difficult as it is to come by these days, she's certain to pick up another job easily."

"Why did you do that, Lis?" Dad asked in surprise. "You know how hard I've been trying to get you to hire on a few extra people to help out around here. Why on earth did you fire the one girl you seemed to find satisfactory?"

"As you know, dear, I feel strongly about my privacy," Lisette said. "I don't at all like the idea of having someone in my employment entertaining her boyfriends here. This 'Dave' person from the roofing crew was over here last week visiting Celina on her worktime. That's the sort of thing I simply won't put up with."

I was resolved that I would not allow her to defeat me.

"Dad," I said, "I'd like to go into Merveille today. Can I take our car?" I put a slight emphasis upon the word *our*. The Pontiac had been, after all, my mother's car. Asking for the use of that was quite different from asking for the Monte Carlo.

"Sure," Dad said easily. "Are you going to be doing some shopping?"

"I want to get some sandals," I told him. "Mine got soaked when I fell in the river, and the soles are coming off."

"Josie, why don't you go with her?" Lisette suggested. "You've been telling me that you need new tennis shoes."

"I've got other things I need to do too," I said, before Josie had a chance to respond. "I'm going to be doing all kinds of stupid errands, and I was planning to spend the whole afternoon at the library. Josie would be bored to death."

"Jo doesn't get bored easily," said Lisette. "She has things she needs to do also. And I'm sure that she'd be happy to go

136

with you to the library. She was just saying yesterday that she's run out of things to read."

"I don't want to have to chauffeur Josie around today," I said, my voice coming out sharper than I had intended. "You're the one who values privacy so much, Lisette. Don't you think that maybe *I* —"

"Don't be ungracious, Nore," my father interrupted. "Lord knows, your mother and I chauffered *you* around enough when you were too young to get your license. Now you can repay us by extending the same favor to your step-sister."

I was familiar enough with my father's stubborn nature to see at once that this was a no-win situation. Any further argument on my part would probably lose me the use of the car altogether. So, the way things ended up, Josie was seated in the front seat next to me when I drove away from Shadow Grove.

I had no intention, however, of letting her remain there. A mile down the road, I pulled over onto the shoulder.

"This is as far as you go," I said. "Now you can get out and walk home."

"What do you mean?" Josie asked, in apparent bewilderment. "I thought we were going to Merveille."

"*I* am going to Merveille," I said. "You're not going with me. I don't trust you anymore, and I don't want your company. And you can stop giving me that innocent, wide-eyed, hurt look. You know perfectly well what Gabe tried to do to me. You were in on the plot just as much as he and your mother were."

"I don't know what you mean," Josie said again, but her eyes avoided mine. "Why would I want bad things to happen to you, Nore? I like you a lot. I'm your friend."

"I think you do like me," I conceded, "but you're not my

137

friend. If you were, you'd have warned me that Gabe was going to try to drown me."

"I didn't know about that," Josie said defensively. "Maman put me to sleep. Nobody told me that it was already time for —" She fell silent, obviously realizing that she had admitted too much.

"Tell me why!" I demanded while she was still off balance. "Tell me why Gabe did it!"

"I can't tell you anything," Josie said nervously. "I just wish you'd never come here, you or your father either. Chuck's a nice man. I bet he was good to your mother. I bet he was faithful to her, and didn't run around on her."

"Of course he was faithful to her," I said. "Dad loved my mother. What does that have to do with anything?"

"My father didn't love Maman," Josie said. "At least, not enough to stay faithful to her. He had a Cajun girlfriend living downriver. When Maman found out about it, she was so hurt and angry she just about went crazy."

"I don't know what you're telling me this for," I said. "I don't care a bit how your father treated your mother. You are right about one thing, though — Dad and I should never have come here." I leaned across her and opened the door on the passenger's side. "Now, get out and go home."

"Please, let me come with you!" Josie said beseechingly. "I won't be any trouble, I promise. Maman will be so mad if I don't."

"Then, let her be mad," I said. "I mean it, Jo — get out! Don't make me have to shove you. I'm bigger and stronger than you are, and you might get hurt."

Josie threw me a startled glance — sat, considering the threat for a moment — and then, apparently deciding that I could, indeed, evict her by force if I chose to, reluctantly climbed out of the car. When I last saw her in the rearview mirror as I drove off, she was walking back along the side of the road in the direction from which we had come. Her shoulders were slumped dejectedly, and she appeared to be in no hurry to get back to the house and face her mother.

Relieved to be alone at last, I kept my mind busy for the next forty miles planning what I would do with my hard-won day of freedom. I decided that my first stop on reaching Merveille would be at the telephone company. When I got there, I registered a complaint about the long amount of time that it was taking to have our phone installed. I was not especially surprised when the people in the office, after a lengthy search of their files, were unable to locate a record of any such order ever having been placed.

After leaving the office itself, I stopped at a pay phone in the lobby to make my call to Celina. It wasn't until I had the phone directory open and was aimlessly flicking through the pages that I suddenly realized that I had forgotten the girl's last name. As I stood there, racking my brain to recall it, it occurred to me that even if I did manage to reach her, it would be doubtful that, having just been fired by my step-mother, Celina would be any too eager to help with a family research project.

That left only one other person I could turn to. Dave Par-lange knew Celina's grandfather and would be able to tell me how to reach him. I felt embarrassed about asking a favor of Dave, after the circumstances of our last awkward encounter, but I could think of no other way to get the information.

Opening the directory to the P's, I found the listing for Parlange Roofing Company and dialed it. He probably wouldn't even be there, I told myself, as I listened to the phone ring on the other end of the line.

This was not the case, however. Within moments after I had identified myself to the woman who answered the phone, Dave was on the line.

"This is a surprise," he said, a trifle coolly. "I thought you didn't have a telephone."

"We don't," I told him. "I'm here in town, calling from a public phone. Dave, I need your help. I have to get in touch with Celina's grandfather."

"With Charlie Lacouture?" Dave said in surprise. "Why is that?"

"I need to ask him —" I began automatically to swing into my story about the research project, and then I paused. I had been desperately wishing that there was someone whom I could confide in. Was it possible that Dave might turn out to be such a person?

"Something's very wrong at Shadow Grove," I said cautiously. "Something's going on there that scares me. Since Mr. Lacouture used to work there, I was hoping that maybe he could help me understand things."

"He lives in an apartment over on Second Street," said Dave. "He's living on Social Security, and I don't think he has a phone."

"I've got to talk to him," I said, my voice shaking a little. "I can't tell you how important it is."

"What's the deal?" Dave asked. The irritation was gone from his voice now. "What's the problem, Nore? What's the thing that's wrong at Shadow Grove? You sound scared to death."

I drew a deep breath and let him have it.

"The people there are trying to kill me," I said.

Even to my own ears, the statement sounded utterly crazy. If my own father wouldn't believe me, how could I expect someone else to, especially someone whom I knew so slightly?

There was a long moment of silence.

Then Dave said quietly, "Where are you calling from? We're between jobs right now, and I've got this afternoon off. I'll come pick you up. The best way to get to old Charlie will be to just stop over there in person."

CHAPTER

14

CHARLIE Lacouture's apartment was on the ground level of a run-down, two-story complex that backed onto a lumberyard. When Dave and I got out of his car, we were greeted by the pungent aroma of newly cut wood and the ear-piercing shriek of a buzz saw.

"That end unit's Charlie's," Dave said. "It's Number Eleven."

Other than for our initial greetings when he had picked me up in the parking lot out behind the telephone company, the two of us had barely spoken. It was as if we were in silent agreement that there was too much that needed to be explained for us to attempt to start the discussion on this short a car trip.

Now, however, as we crossed the patch of weed-covered lawn that separated the line of apartments from the parking area, Dave did suddenly start to talk.

"Charlie's in his seventies, but he's sharp as a tack," he

said. "He's like a walking encyclopedia when it comes to trivia. I'd better warn you, once you get him going, he's going to talk your ear off."

"That's fine with me," I said. "There's a lot I'd like to hear about."

"Like what?" Dave asked me. "He hasn't been out to Shadow Grove for thirty years or more. I can't believe that he could have anything to tell you that would pertain to what's going on there today."

"That's where you're wrong," I said. "The most recent years aren't the ones that I'm really concerned about. I know where the family was during that span of time. What I do need to know is who was living at Shadow Grove and what was going on there in the years before that."

There was no response the first few times that Dave pushed the door bell. I was just beginning to accept that Charlie Lacouture was out and that my trip into town would turn out to be a wasted one, when the door was pulled open a crack and a gruff voice asked, "What do you want?"

"It's Dave Parlange, Charlie," Dave said. "I've got a friend with me. We were in the neighborhood and thought we'd stop by and say 'hi.' "

"Dave — well, hello, boy!" The man's tone of voice changed abruptly from suspicious to welcoming. The main door was yanked open all the way, and a deeply grooved face, topped by a shock of snowy hair, appeared behind the screen.

"Well, this is something!" Charlie Lacouture said with obvious pleasure, as he wrestled with the latch and finally got the screen door open. "I'm right glad to see you, boy! Haven't had any company, except for family, all week long! Who's this you've got with you — the newest girlfriend?"

143

"This is Nore Robbins," Dave told him, stepping back so that I could enter the apartment ahead of him. As we stepped into the tiny efficiency, heat came billowing out to meet us as though it had been released from a blast furnace. The living room–kitchenette combination would have been totally dark if it had not been for the illumination supplied by one naked light bulb, set into the center of the ceiling. Two of the three small windows had blinds pulled over them, and the third held a small electric fan that was laboring futilely to stir the stifling air into some sort of motion.

"I know it's stuffy in here," Charlie said apologetically, as he motioned us toward the faded love seat, whose rusted springs hung beneath it like the udders of a cow. Two equally shabby, mismatched chairs completed the room's meager furnishings. "I don't have no choice, though, about keeping things sealed up. Breathing in that sawdust don't do nothing good for these old lungs." He took his own seat in one of the chairs, and Dave and I sat down on the sagging love seat. "So, it's Nore Robbins, is it? You got good taste, boy. This your serious sweetie?"

"Well, we haven't exactly set the date yet," Dave said lightly. "Nore's dad just got married to the lady who owns the old Bergé place, and Nore's here visiting for the summer."

"Yep — Robbins. That's the name my granddaughter told me — Robbins. I knew it wasn't Bergé no more, but those names keep changing so fast out there, it's hard to keep track of them." Charlie settled back in his chair. "Celina's not working there no more, she tells me. That's just as well, I say. It's too big a place for one lone girl to keep up."

"Yes," I agreed awkwardly, "it's an awfully big house. I'm sure there are lots of jobs Celina will like better."

"Back when I was working there, they had themselves a houseful of help," Charlie said. "Mr. Vardeman — he insisted on that — no matter what the missus said about wanting her privacy and all. A cook, they had, and two maids, if I remember right, and there was three of us gardeners and a stablehand who didn't do nothing except look after all them horses."

"Vardeman?" Dave said. "That name doesn't ring any bells with me. All I've ever heard the house referred to is 'the Bergé place.' "

"That's all anybody's ever called it since the late eighteen hundreds," Charlie said. "The rich DuBois family owned that place back in Civil War days, but they gave it to their daughter as a wedding gift when she got married to Henri Bergé. It was a cotton plantation then, and supposed to've been a good one. Henri and his wife died somewhere around nineteen twenty or so, and the house set empty for years and got all run down. Then the granddaughter — a widow with three children — moved back there, and she married this man named Robert Vardeman. That was Depression times, but Mr. Vardeman wasn't hurting none; he had a little automobile company and sold out to General Motors or some such thing. Anyway, he had a bunch of money and got the place fixed up. That's when I was hired on there to take care of the grounds."

"She had three children?" I asked, trying to keep my excitement from showing in my voice. "Were they little? I mean, were any of them babies?"

"Nope," the old man said. "They was all of them teenagers, two boys and a girl. I never saw much of the boys. They was always off together someplace, fishing or riding their horses. The girl, little Josephine, I did see plenty of her.

She was a friendly kid. She'd come out and hang around when I was working on the flower beds and chat away at me. I was a young man then and, if I do say so myself, not hurting none in the looks department. The girl, Josie, she just kept buzzing around me like a little mosquito. Her mother didn't like that, I can tell you, not one little bit. Those people was both of them real protective about their children."

"Vardeman was only their stepfather, wasn't he?" Dave asked.

"He was that, yes, the kids went by the family name, Bergé. But Mr. Vardeman, he was a real goodhearted man, and he loved them kids. I heard him once, talking to the missus, just like he was those children's real dad. He wanted her to take them to town to see a doctor."

"A doctor!" I exclaimed. "Why? What was he worried about?"

"He just didn't think they was growing right," Charlie said. "Especially the girl. She was sort of a pet of his. 'That Josie hasn't grown an inch in the three years since we've been married,' I heard him say one day. 'The boys haven't either. None of them's filling out like they ought to at their ages. I think they all three of them ought to get checkups.' " Charlie picked up a folded sheet of newspaper and began to fan himself. "Wish that fan would do a better job. It sure gets close in here. You folks want some water or something?"

"That would taste good," Dave said. Perspiration was streaming down his face. "Don't get up; I'll get some for all of us. You go ahead with your story, Charlie. You're talking about the early nineteen thirties, aren't you?"

"Let's see now — it was nineteen thirty-three or so, I think." Charlie closed his eyes a moment in concentration.

Then he opened them and nodded. "Yep, that was the very year. I remember because my wife and I had just started courting. We was married one year later, in nineteen thirty-four. That's why we was away in New Orleans when Mr. Vardeman had his accident. We was on our honeymoon."

"He had an accident?" I asked, my heart beating faster. "What sort of accident? Was he hurt badly?"

"Bad as you can get," Charlie said. "My mother-in-law, she saved the clippings from the paper so my wife and me could read all about it when we got back. It seems like he and one of the boys was out fishing on the river, and the boat tipped over. The boy swum in to shore okay, but his stepdad drowned. I always thought that was a pretty odd thing to have happened. Mr. Vardeman, he was a good swimmer. In the summer, he swum in that river all the time."

Dave, who had filled his own glass from the faucet in the kitchenette and drained it with one gulp, now came back into the living room, carrying glasses of water for Charlie and me. He handed them to us and again took his seat next to me on the love seat.

"Thanks," I told him, taking a grateful swallow of the tepid liquid. Then, turning my full attention back to Charlie, I asked, "What did the family do then? Did they continue to live at Shadow Grove or did they move away?"

"It's funny you'd think to ask that," Charlie said. "They did move away. The missus, she inherited a lot of money, I guess, from Mr. Vardeman, and she decided to take the kids and do some traveling. She put the place with some caretaking service, and the family moved up North to New England or some such place. They never came back neither, except for one of them."

"Which one was that?" Dave asked, whether out of politeness or real curiosity I couldn't tell.

"The girl," Charlie said. "Some fifteen years later, she came back, all growed up. She'd been married and divorced, and now *she* had three children. She got married to a rich fellow named Mr. Zollenger."

"Who got Shadow Grove 'all fixed up'?" I suggested.

"Yep, he did that," said Charlie, "but then a sad thing happened. One of the boys got throwed by a horse and was killed. Rumor had it his mother took that mighty hard. Soon after that, there was another tragedy. Mr. Zollenger, he got himself killed in some sort of freak accident. Then, the mother took the two kids that she still got left, and the three of them went away somewhere together."

"And a number of years later, her grown daughter returned to Shadow Grove with *her* two children," I said softly, able to complete the history without his help. "And *she* got married to a rich man, and *he* had an accident."

Charlie nodded. "His name was Hillerman, I believe."

I did not need to hear any more. The rest of the story was predictable. There was still something further, however, that I needed to know.

I opened my purse and took out the photograph that I had found in Gabe's bureau and handed it across to Charlie.

"This is a picture I found at Shadow Grove," I said. "I think the people in it used to live there. Do you happen to recognize any of them?"

"Sure do," the old man said, squinting at the photograph with faded blue eyes. "That's Mrs. Vardeman right there. Right pretty woman, she was. She's dressed sort of old-fashioned, but except for that, she looks just the way she did when I was working for her. And those are her kids, Mr. Gabriel and Mr. Louis and Miss Josephine."

"And the man?" I asked. "Who is he? Is that Mr. Vardeman?

"Oh, no," Charlie said with certainty. "Mr. Vardeman wasn't old like that. I don't recall ever seeing this man around the place. Truth was, nobody much was ever around except for the people who worked there. The missus, she had a real thing about what she called her 'privacy.' It was like she was scared folks was going to get into her things. She made her husband get one of the cabins out behind the house all boarded up and padlocked, and she kept all her papers and private stuff out there."

"Can I see the picture?" Dave asked with interest.

He took the photograph from Charlie and sat for a moment, studying it.

"Whew!" he said finally, giving a soft, surprised whistle. "Talk about family resemblance! The girl and the older boy in this picture are the spitting images of Josie and Gabe!"

"I know," I said faintly. I had learned so much so quickly that my head felt ready to burst with newfound knowledge. I took a gulp of my water and closed my eyes tightly, willing the world to stop spinning so that I could think.

"What's the matter?" Dave asked. "You look like you're ready to keel over."

"I'm sorry," I whispered. "It's the heat, I guess. Coming from the North, I'm just not used to it."

"It hits lots of people like that," Charlie said sympathetically. "I'm used to it myself, but I still don't like it none. Maybe you'd best take her outside, Dave, so she can get some air."

"I'll do that," Dave said, getting up and extending his hand to me. "Actually, I guess we need to get going anyway. Thanks for the visit, Charlie. We sure enjoyed it."

"Yes," I managed to say, as Dave pulled me gently to my

149

feet. "Yes, thank you for your stories. You'll never know how interesting they were to me."

"You come back any time," Charlie said warmly. "There's a million more that I can tell you." He got up and came to the door with us to see us out. "You bring her back again, boy, but in the morning next time so it'll be cooler. It's right nice to have some visitors to talk to."

As Dave and I stepped out into the brilliance of overhead sunlight, the heat of midday seemed almost refreshing compared to Charlie's apartment. With his hand on my arm, Dave steered me over to his car, opened the door for me, and then went around to get in on the driver's side. I leaned back against the seat and drew in a deep breath of fresh, unfettered air, thankful that we had been sensible enough to have left the windows open.

"So, did you get what you came for?" Dave asked me, as he started the engine.

"Yes," I told him. I knew that he expected more from me, but I could not think what to say.

"So, give it a run-through," Dave commanded. "What exactly came out of that? Charlie gave us a whole lot of background on Shadow Grove, but what does it mean? You said on the phone that somebody's trying to kill you. What connection does all this history have with *that?*"

"You wouldn't believe me if I told you," I said softly.

"So — try me."

"All right." I accepted the challenge. "What 'came out of' Charlie's stories was one basic unit — a beautiful, young widow and her children. When Charlie Lacouture worked at Shadow Grove, over fifty years ago, they were living there with the woman's rich, new husband. The husband died and left his wife his money, and the family moved away. One generation later, the girl in the family came back again with *her* teenage children. She got married to somebody rich, and *her* husband died, and she and her kids moved away. Then one generation later, it all happened over again. Doesn't that strike you as a tremendous amount of coincidence?"

"It's strange," Dave agreed. "But what *could* it be but coincidence?"

"A plan," I said. "A carefully fashioned plan. It could be a plan that has worked so well for this family that they've used it over and over down through the years."

"A plan that involves killing people off for their money?" Dave turned to stare across at me incredulously. "That's crazy, Nore. That's not to say that it couldn't have happened once. From what Charlie said, that boating accident did sound fishy, and if Vardeman had just sold his car business to General Motors, his wife must have stood to inherit a heap. What *you're* talking about, though, is one family after another, all doing the exact same terrible thing."

"No, it's not," I said. "What I'm talking about is just one family, doing the exact same thing a number of times. I'm talking about a family with a secret, and that secret is that *none of them ever age.*"

"That's impossible," Dave said.

"I told you, you wouldn't believe me."

"How can I believe a crazy thing like that?"

"You can't," I said. "You aren't close enough to it to see it. To believe it, you would have to be living at Shadow Grove. You would have to catch these people in the little mistakes they make. Josie, for instance, once told me that she remembered living in Connecticut, because she was in Hartford at the time the Ringling circus tent caught fire."

"She couldn't have been," Dave said logically. "Everybody's read about that fire. It occurred more than forty years ago."

"That's exactly what I mean!" How could I convince him! "What about the picture? Charlie said that the people in it were living at Shadow Grove when he was working there. I don't believe that photograph was taken then. My parents' baby pictures were taken in the 'thirties. They're printed on regular paper like what's used today. This picture was printed on some sort of old-time metal plating. I'll bet you anything it was taken years before the woman in it married Robert Vardeman. I'll bet that old man was her first husband and the children's real father, Henri Bergé."

"You can talk forever, and I still won't believe you, Nore," Dave said. "It's not that I don't want to, it's just that what you're saying is impossible. There's got to be some explanation other than the one you're suggesting." As though in apology, he reached over and covered my hand with his. "What I *do* believe is that you're scared out of your mind. And, since you don't come across as the hysterical type, I can only figure that there's something going on out at Shadow Grove that's really creepy. I want to help you if I can, just as long as you don't keep trying to tell me that everybody out there except you and your father is a hundred years old."

"All right," I said. "I won't try to tell you that."

"So, what is it that you want me to do?" Dave asked.

"Nothing quite yet," I told him. "The first step has to be mine. I'm going to try to get into that locked-up storeroom. If what Charlie says is right, there's going to be stuff in there that will answer a lot of my questions. Depending on what I find there, we can figure out what our next step should be."

"Since you don't have a phone, how are we going to communicate?" Dave asked.

"Why don't you drive out tomorrow night and pick me up?" I said. "I'll tell Dad and Lisette we're going to the movies."

"So, I do get a date after all!" Dave commented wryly. "I get off work at five, so I can be out at Shadow Grove around six or so. You're sure that you're not going to end up being 'busy'?"

"I turned you down last time because I didn't want to hurt Josie," I said. "Right now, hurting any of these people's feelings is the last thing I'm going to worry about."

CHAPTER

-⚜️ 15 ⚜️-

Having had neither breakfast nor lunch that day, I stopped at a drive-in for a hamburger and milk shake, and I didn't get back to Shadow Grove until ten past four. My two-member reception committee was awaiting me in the parlor. As I came in the front door, I could look straight across and see them there — Dad and Lisette, side by side on the sofa — with fire in their eyes.

"Nore, come in here this minute!" Dad called out to me as I made a furtive attempt to slip past them and continue on up to my room without stopping to speak.

Reluctantly, I turned back and went into the parlor.

"What is it?" I asked guardedly.

"You know the answer to that as well as I do," said Dad. "I can't believe that a daughter of mine would behave as you did this morning. What you did to poor little Josie was inexcusable."

"I don't see that I did anything all that terrible," I said. "I

154

let her out of the car no more than a mile down the road. She hardly had to walk any distance at all."

"The length of the distance she walked has nothing to do with this," Dad said. "You promised to take Josie to Merveille, and you went back on your word."

"I didn't promise anything," I objected. "I told you from the beginning that I didn't want to take her."

"And I told *you* that you *had* to!" Dad said, his voice rising. "I gave you the use of the car on that condition. What did you do there all day anyway? I don't see any shoe box."

"I shopped all morning, but I couldn't find what I wanted," I said. "Then I had lunch and spent the afternoon at the library."

"That's not true, Nore," said Lisette. "Your father checked at the library, and you weren't there."

"How could he have checked at the library when we don't have a phone?" I demanded. "And, while we're on that subject, I did some checking today myself. The people at the phone company say that you never ordered a telephone at all. No wonder it's taking them so long to get around to installing it!"

"Don't you dare talk to Lisette that way, young lady!" Dad said angrily. "I checked the library in person, not by phone. I had a letter from my agent this morning asking me to fly to New York to meet with my publisher on Friday. *Because* we don't have a phone, I had to drive into town to make a plane reservation. While I was there, I stopped by the library to try to locate you. The librarian said that you hadn't been there all day."

"Didn't you hear what I just said?" I asked him. "Lisette lied to you, Dad! She never even tried to get a phone installed! She doesn't want us to be able to call out from here!

155

If we could do that, she wouldn't be able to control things!"

Lisette flinched as though I had struck her physically.

"Oh, Chuck!" she said softly, her lovely eyes filling with tears. "How can she say such things? I've tried so hard to get her to like me!"

"You've said quite enough, Nore." Dad was obviously struggling to hold himself under control. "Despite what you may think, you are not too old to be sent to your room. I want you to go upstairs and stay there until dinnertime. When you do come down, you're to apologize to both Lisette and Josie."

"Over my dead body!" I retorted and was halfway up the stairs before I realized the significance of what I'd said. When I did, a shiver ran through me as if I'd suddenly been hit by a blast of icy air. Continuing on to the top of the stairs and down the hall to my room, I entered it and closed the door. Then, with my own words ringing in my ears, I turned back to punch the button in the center of the knob. Immediately, I realized how futile that gesture would be. The French doors had no latches, and since all the bedrooms on the second floor opened onto a common balcony, anybody was free to come into my room at any time, whether the door to the hall was locked or not.

Crossing over to the bureau, I picked up the picture of my mother and stood for many moments, drinking in the wholesome sweetness of her laugh-lined face. After eighteen years of marriage to a woman like this one, how could my father possibly have chosen Lisette! "You aren't close enough to see it," I had said to Dave, when he had refused to believe my accusations about the Bergé family. "To believe it, you would have to be living at Shadow Grove." But my father *was* living at Shadow Grove! He had been exposed to all the same things that I had! How could he be so blind that he couldn't recognize the fact that something was sick and frightening and terribly wrong?

Because he was in love.

It was that simple. Dad was in love with Lisette, just as other men had been before him — the Mr. Hillerman whom Charlie had mentioned, Mr. Zollenger and Robert Vardeman. And what about her first husband, Henri Bergé? Had *he* loved Lisette? According to Josie, Bergé had hurt his wife badly by becoming involved with a young Cajun woman. Knowing this, it was easier now for me to understand Lisette's seemingly senseless prejudice against Cajun people in general and the women in particular.

Setting the picture of my mother back on the bureau, I went over to the bed and stretched out on top of the spread. Lying there, staring at the ceiling, I ran through in my mind all the events of the day, starting with my conversation with Josie in the car. Josie had not denied that her brother had attempted to drown me, only that she herself had been involved in the scheme. "I didn't know about that," she had said. "Maman put me to sleep. Nobody told me it was time yet."

It was the passage of time that was somehow the key to everything. If — as I was now convinced, despite what common sense might dictate — Lisette, Gabe, and Josie had survived for over a century without any physical signs of aging, this could be explained only by the fact that they had discovered some process by which they had been able to alter their relationship to time. Josie's hysterical words that one afternoon in the courtyard came rushing back to me — "Time keeps going by, but it just doesn't count!" At that point, I had not understood what it was that she meant by that. Now, I was very much afraid that I did.

What, though, about the other two members of the family? There were five people in the photograph I had found in Gabe's bureau. If the elderly man in the picture was the children's father, then his physical clock must have continued running in a normal manner in contrast to those of his wife and children. As for the boy, Louis — he had been killed in a riding accident — so if the Bergé family had, indeed, discovered the secret of eternal *youth,* this evidently was not synonymous with eternal *life.*

My brain was reeling with the weight of such incredible concepts. As Dave had said, they were all impossible. Yet, when I closed my eyes and slipped into dreaming, I heard my mother's voice say quietly, "Believe them, Nore."

I had slept so little the night before that now when sleep did hit me, I went totally under. Since I had no intention of apologizing to Lisette and Josie, I did not set my mental alarm clock to wake me at dinnertime and slept straight through the evening until almost midnight.

What woke me at last was a sound. It was not a loud sound, but it was one that I must have been subconsciously braced for, for in one instant's time I came totally awake, with every muscle tense and my heart pounding.

At first I was not sure exactly what it was that I'd heard. After a moment, though, the sound came again, and this time I did know. It was someone turning the knob of my door.

There was no time in which to form a real plan. The one thing that flew into my mind was that I must not remain in the most predictable place. As silently as possible, I slipped out of bed and moved across the room to flatten myself against the wall next to the bureau. Although I could not see into the pocket of darkness at the end of the room, I sensed movement there as the door came silently open. A moment later, I heard the faint brush of bare feet against hardwood floorboards and saw a black shape emerge from the darkness to become outlined against the moonlit sky beyond the balcony doors.

Raising my right hand to the bureau top, I began to grope cautiously along it in search of something that could be used as a weapon. My fingers soundlessly worked their way past Mother's picture, past a box of Kleenex and a stack of cassette tapes, and settled around the handle of my plastic hairdryer. It was not the sturdiest thing in the world with which to enter combat, but with the element of surprise on my side, it seemed possible that I might be able to wield it hard enough to stun somebody, at least momentarily.

Gripping the dryer tightly, I lifted it high above my head and was just preparing to lunge forward and bring it crashing down on the figure beside the bed, when a familiar voice asked softly, "Nore? Are you awake?"

It was all that I could do to keep my knees from buckling beneath me as the tension went out of me in one great rush. Slowly, I let the hand that held the dryer sink to my side.

"Yes, Josie, I'm awake," I said. "It's a good thing for you that you spoke up when you did. In another minute you'd have had your head smashed in."

I stepped over to the bedside table and turned on the light.

Josie whirled to face me, a startled expression on her face. She was dressed in pink baby doll pajamas, and her skinny legs protruded from beneath them like knobby match sticks. The childish flatness of her chest was accentuated by the clinging fabric, and her chin was coated with a chalky white acne medication. She was holding something bunched up in her right hand.

"Why aren't you in bed?" she squeaked. "What are you doing over there?"

159

"Trying to keep from being murdered," I told her cryptically. "Considering what happened on the river the other day, can you really blame me for getting nervous when somebody comes creeping into my room at night?"

"I needed to talk to you," Josie said.

"Then why didn't you knock?"

"I didn't want Gabe to hear me."

"That's a good story, Jo," I said. "It's a pity I don't believe it."

"But it's true!" Josie insisted. "I know Maman and your father are sleeping hard, because I gave them the sleepytime anisette, but Gabe's light is still on. I saw it through the crack under the door."

"You gave our parents the special anisette!" I exclaimed. "I thought Gabe kept that in *his* room!"

"He does," Josie said. "He keeps the bottle under his mattress, but I sneaked in this afternoon and poured some into a jelly jar."

"And gave it to our parents after dinner?" I regarded her incredulously. "Why did you do that? Surely you're not planning to go out someplace at this hour!"

"I wanted them to sleep so I could go into their room," said Josie. "There was something in Maman's purse I wanted to get for you."

"What's that?" I asked. "A dose of arsenic?"

"That's not fair, Nore," Josie said in an injured voice. "I haven't done anything bad to you, so don't be so mean. See what I brought you!"

She extended her hand and opened the balled-up first. In it there was a roll of bills.

"Money?" I said in surprise. "What do I need money for?"

"It's almost three hundred dollars." She continued to thrust it out at me. "Go on, Nore, take it. It's enough to buy yourself a plane ticket."

"A plane ticket to where?"

"It doesn't matter," Josie said. "Just anywhere. Run away someplace where nobody can find you."

"Like L.A.," I said. "That's Gabe's line. He asked me to run away with him to California where we could live together and work as movie extras and have a high old time. Then five minutes later he tried to kill me. Is that what you're going to do? While I'm counting the money are you planning to turn around and stick a knife between my ribs?"

"Of course not," Josie said. "I just want to help you. And Gabe must have, too, or he wouldn't have tried to get you to go away. If you told him no, then that was your fault. There's just so much that he and I can do for people."

"Josie," I said softly, "you're incredible. I can't believe what I just heard you say. There's 'just so much' that you and your brother can do between murders!"

"I didn't say that," said Josie, sounding shocked. "I never, ever told you a thing like that. You're the one who keeps using words like *kill* and *murder*. All I said was that I know that you're feeling unhappy here. I thought that maybe I could help you get away."

"I don't want your mother's money," I told her bitterly. "Much as I do want to leave Shadow Grove, I am certainly not going to walk out on my unsuspecting father and leave him here to be eaten alive by his black widow wife."

"Your father will be all right," Josie said matter-of-factly. "Nothing can happen to him, Nore, as long as you're alive someplace and nobody knows where."

"Nothing will *happen* to him!" I exclaimed. "I'll just *bet* it

161

won't! Just the way nothing happened to —" I caught myself before I could blurt out the name of Robert Vardeman. There was no sense in disclosing to Josie at this point how much I had found out about her family history. This was information that I would use later as ammunition with which to convince my father.

"So you're not going to go?" Josie asked me.

"No, I'm not," I said. "Not until Dad agrees to go with me, which he will very soon. So, go stick that money back in your dear mother's purse. You can be sure she's going to need every penny of it when Dad files for divorce."

"Okay," Josie said. "Just remember that I did really try."

She crossed to the door, placed her hand on the knob, and then turned back to face me. For a moment she simply stood there in silence.

Then she said in a rush, "You have to understand how it is with us, Nore. It's not the same as with other families. We may not agree with the things she does — we may even sometimes hate her — but there's no way Gabe and I could do without Maman. She's the only grown-up we have." She paused, and then added in a less impassioned voice, "Turn out the light so it won't show out into the hall."

I reached over and flicked off the bedside lamp. In the sudden flood of darkness, I heard the door open and then softly close.

Moving away from the bed, I went over to the door and stood with my ear pressed against it. It was over five minutes before I heard the sound of the door of Josie's room being opened and shut. I could only suppose that she had used the intervening time to go back to our parents' bedroom and return the pilfered money to her mother's wallet.

For the next ten minutes I continued to stand without

moving, waiting to see if any other sounds would be forth-coming. When none were, and I felt certain that Josie was settled in for the night, I opened my own door and stepped out into the hall. As I walked slowly down it, trailing my fin-gertips along the wall for guidance, I was relieved to see that the strip of light that Josie had commented on having sighted under Gabe's door was no longer in evidence.

When I reached the door to the bedroom that was shared by Dad and Lisette, I opened it quickly, before I could lose my nerve, and stepped inside. After the total darkness of the hallway, the moonlit interior seemed incredibly bright. Light streamed in through the door to the balcony to fall in great splashes of silver upon the Oriental rug and the an-tique dressing table and to illuminate the two sleeping fig-ures that lay side by side on the double bed.

My father was lying flat on his back with his mouth slightly open, snoring. Lisette lay on her left side with her back turned toward him. She, too, was breathing heavily with the slow, steady rhythm that accompanies deep slum-ber. The sleepytiime anisette had done its job.

I did not have to turn on the light to locate Lisette's purse. It was lying on the dressing table in a pool of moonlight. Going directly over to it, I undid the clasp and opened it. Bypassing the wallet, which was situated near the top, I groped down into its depths until my hand closed around the object that I had come for — a metal ring that held a large assortment of keys.

CHAPTER

16

THE courtyard was filled with moonlight when I crossed it to reach the line of cabins behind the house. I gazed up at the globe of light above me and was disconcerted to realize that this round, white face had looked down upon the world since its creation. On a night over one hundred years ago, this very same moon might have witnessed the birth of a baby girl named Lisette DuBois who later grew up to become Lisette Bergé. It had seen the birth of Lisette and Henri's three children, and many years later, the death of one of their sons. Somewhere in between these two events, it might have even observed whatever had taken place that had kept the Bergé family from ever growing old.

Tonight, I told myself, I, too, would learn that secret. For some undefined reason, I was filled with a strange sort of certainty that somewhere within the cabin Lisette used as a storage room there lay information that was going to explain the unexplainable.

Finding the key to fit the lock to that cabin was no easy matter, as Lisette had more than two dozen keys on her ring. There were house keys and car keys (I recognized a set that belonged to my mother's Pontiac), suitcase keys and tiny keys designed for such things as diaries and jewelry boxes, multiple no-name keys that might have been made to open almost anything, and one huge brass key which I could only imagine must fit the giant lock on the gate at the end of the driveway.

Once I did finally manage to locate the key to the storage cabin, it turned easily in the padlock. I pulled the lock free so that the door could swing open, and reached inside to grope along the wall for a light switch.

By the time it occurred to me that slave quarters would not have been wired for electricity, my fingers did locate a switch, and the room was filled with light. The fact that someone in more recent years had taken the trouble to have had electricity installed seemed to me to be a good indication that the cabin was being visited with some frequency.

I pulled the door closed behind me and turned to face the room. My whole first impression was of being surrounded by the past. This feeling was not the result of the appearance of the piles of documents, photographs, books and ledgers that covered every inch of floor space so much as it was the smell of them. The musty odor of aged paper was so overwhelming that my eyes were watering before I had even had a chance to focus them. Once I did zero in on the room's total contents, I stopped thinking about anything except the magnitude of the huge reservoir of material that lay before me.

Unable to contemplate an organized investigation of so much written matter, I leaned over and picked up the item closest to my hand. This turned out to be a folder filled with marriage certificates. As I leafed through its contents, the names that leapt out at me were familiar ones. The oldest of the certificates documented the fact that in the year 1877 Henri Louis Bergé had been joined in wedlock to Lisette DuBois. Next in the pile, there was a certificate legalizing the 1931 marriage of Lisette DuBois Bergé to Robert Vardeman. Doing some quick mental arithmetic, I managed to ascertain that even if Lisette had been in her teens at the time of her first marriage, by the year 1931 she would have had to have been close to seventy years old.

I flipped through the remainder of the documents, filing the names and dates in my memory for future reference. Zollenger and Hillerman were there, as well as two other names which Charlie Lacouture had neglected to mention — Stephen Donaldson and William Buchanan. These most recent of Lisette's ill-fated husbands had evidently come and gone with so little fanfare that the normally observant Charlie had not known of their existence. Dad's and Lisette's certificate was not among those in the folder, and I could only imagine that Dad must have it in his own possession.

For the next several hours, I worked my way methodically through masses of letters, pictures and legal documents, not certain what it was I was searching for, but feeling sure that I would know it when I found it. Some of the papers I found meaningful; others were more confusing than enlightening. Among those falling into that latter category were the financial statements, receipts, bank books and investment materials. These were so numerous and so out of order that it was hard to imagine even a full-time accountant being able to make any sense of them in a lifetime.

Some of my more interesting finds as a result of my investigation were death certificates for Lisette's son, Louis, and for her husbands Norman Zollenger and William Buchanan. Louis was listed as having died of a broken neck in 1941. Zollender had died of "unknown causes" in 1950, and Buchanan had suffered a drowning death in 1964. These papers turned up separately, instead of grouped together in one folder, which seemed to indicate that the certificates recording the deaths of Lisette's earlier husbands were likely to be scattered about in other areas of the room.

The photographs were better organized. Most of these were stored in manila envelopes marked with dates and geographic locations. The older photographs were formally posed, black-and-white studio portraits, but from 1940 on, more and more of the pictures were color snapshots. Out of curiosity, I opened the envelope marked with the year of my birth. Even though I now knew the circumstances of the Bergés' bizarre situation, it still came as a shock to me to riffle through its contents and find a snapshot showing thirteen-year-old Josie feeding peanuts to the elephants at the Memphis Zoo at what might have been the very moment that I was being born.

It was in a far corner of the room, in a cardbard packing box, that I found the seventeen-volume set of leatherbound notebooks. When I opened the first of these, I saw that it had been used as a diary. Recognizing the handwriting as the same delicate, spidery script that Lisette used when making our her shopping lists, I knew immediately that she was the one who had kept the journal.

The paper was yellow and brittle with age, but the ink was still dark enough to be legible. The date of the first of the entries was January 7, 1878.

"This was the most joyous day of my life!" Lisette had

written. "How one's values change when one enters the state of motherhood! On my sixteenth birthday, when dear Henri proposed marriage, I was certain that I would never be happier than on that day. I felt the same on our wedding day when my parents presented me with Shadow Grove. Today, however, I have experienced the ultimate joy. At six twenty-two this morning, after a long and difficult labor, I gave birth to a seven-pound son — Gabriel DuBois Bergé!"

So, here, at last, I had the evidence that I had been searching for! The date of Gabe's nineteeth-century birth was documented in Lisette's own handwriting.

I laid that book aside and, bypassing the next in the series, picked up the volume dated 1880. Here, in an entry made on the third of June, I read of the birth of the Bergés' second son, Louis Henri. Then, in a later edition of my stepmother's chronicles, I read of the birth of Josephine Marie Bergé on April 22, 1882.

From that point on, I thumbed haphazardly through volume after volume, reading a paragraph here and a paragraph there at random. Although "dear Henri" was obviously being subsidized by his wife's wealthy parents, the plantation seemed to be prospering under his management. These early books were filled with references to dinner parties and formal dances, to the fittings of new gowns and to the gifts of jewelry bestowed upon Lisette by her adoring husband. There were lengthy accounts of the playful antics of the Bergé children, including one story about how Gabe and Louis had cavorted in the lily pond and then rushed into the parlor to muddy the furniture. There were also numerous pages in which Lisette rhapsodized dreamily about the "sweet nights" spent in Henri's arms.

Along about 1890, however, the tone of the entries

changed abruptly and took a sudden turn toward depression. Lisette had now celebrated her thirtieth birthday, and although this event had been commemorated with a party and she had received a diamond necklace from her parents, she was deeply concerned about having rounded the traumatic corner that led into what she referred to as her "middle years."

"Life is passing me by too quickly!" she lamented. "I sat for an hour this morning, studying my face in the mirror. The soft roundness is gone from my cheeks, and tiny lines are beginning to form at the corners of my eyes. I am worried that Henri may no longer find me desirable. Although I am still admired at parties, I am dreading that inevitable day when the eyes of my dinner partners dart past me to younger women. Gabriel will soon be entering young manhood, and Louis is almost as tall as I am. My baby, Josie, is pleading for permission to wear her hair up. Soon — soon — I shall be old! Dear Lord, how will I bear it!"

The next several journals continued to take Lisette on a downhill roll, as she became more and more obsessed with the fear of aging. There were reports of trips into New Orleans to purchase imported skin creams and lotions, of beauty masks applied to her face each afternoon at siesta time, and of expensive cosmetics designed to camouflage lines and blemishes. Her jealousy of Henri also seemed to be increasing. Each day's entry culminated with a notation about whether or not he had been home for dinner that night. If the couple attended a party, Lisette would list by name each of the women with whom Henri had chatted, and all of his out-of-town business trips were greeted with suspicion.

Her greatest concern was about the rumor that, once their

wives lost their dewy youthfulness, many of the Creole plantation owners were being "drawn from their homes by spells and potions" to form romantic unions with those young Cajun women who had intermarried with the Cubans and taken up voodoo.

"The wives turn their heads and pretend they don't see," Lisette wrote bitterly. "They fear that to speak out in protest might jeopardize their marriages. No DuBois woman would permit herself to be so humiliated! If I were ever to discover that Henri were engaged in infidelity, I would put an immediate end to either the affair or Henri."

Beginning to realize the direction in which the true-life drama was headed, I hastily picked up the final volume, dated 1895. Turning to the date of Josie's thirteenth birthday, I read Lisette's entry, which described a party at which her daughter had worn her hair piled high on her head and had been allowed to drink champagne: "The only member of the family to miss the celebration was her father, who was called away on supposedly important business. My mother later informed me of the rumors that have been circulating about what Henri's business appointments have recently consisted of. Tomorrow I will pay a call upon a certain woman. I do not believe that my husband will have 'business' in her home again."

As I finished reading this entry and was preparing to turn the page, I was suddenly struck with the realization that it was almost five. Dawn would soon be breaking, which meant that Gabe would be getting up for his morning run. As much as I hated to interrupt my reading, I knew that it would be foolhardy to remain in the cabin any longer. Not only could I not afford a meeting with Gabe on my way back to the house, but I needed to return Lisette's keys to her purse before she and Dad woke up.

Reluctantly, I closed the diary and hauled myself to my feet. My neck was stiff and sore, and the vertebrae in my back seemed welded into place from having remained in one position for so many hours.

On my way to the door, I stooped to gather up the collection of certificates that documented Lisette's many marriages. Then I switched off the light, and with the papers and journal clutched tightly in one hand, I opened the door and stepped out into the dew-drenched world of impending morning.

I replaced the padlock, taking care to position it in such a way that it would not be apparent to a casual observer that it had not been fully closed. Then I crossed the courtyard to the house. Although the moon had by this time completed its course across the sky, there was enough pearly light now seeping in from the sky in the east to allow me to see where I was going.

I let myself into the house and hurried up the stairs and down the hall to Dad and Lisette's bedroom. Without a flood of moonlight to illuminate it, the room was dark enough so that I had to grope my way across it to the dressing table. Locating the purse by touch, I hastily dropped the key ring into it, nervously aware of the altered breathing patterns of the room's two occupants. I had no idea how long the effects of Josie's anisette could be expected to last, but Lisette was already turning restlessly on her pillow and my father was no longer snoring. As I was starting to leave, Dad spoke out sharply in his sleep, and I knew that I had not completed my mission a moment too soon.

I had a second fright when I was almost to my bedroom. Suddenly, I heard the sound of a door being opened at the far end of the hall. Not pausing to glance behind me, I quickened my pace until I was almost running, grabbed the knob of my own door, and threw it open. Plunging into my room, I shoved the door closed behind me and sank down onto the bed.

What, I asked myself, was going to happen next? Had Gabe seen me, or hadn't he? And, if he had, would he suspect where I had been? From my location in the corridor, it should have been obvious that I had not been returning from a trip to the bathroom.

For what seemed an eternity, I sat trembling in anticipation of a rap on my door, or, worse still, of having the door fly open and being confronted with both Gabe and his mother. Eventually, though, as time went by and neither of these events occurred, my heart began to beat more quietly. Impossible as it seemed, perhaps the hallway had been dark enough so that Gabe had come out of his room and still managed to miss me.

More time passed, and my panic gradually subsided. Finally, throwing caution to the winds, I turned on the bedside lamp, reopened the diary, and resumed reading at the point at which I had left off.

The journal's final entry was longer than any of those that had preceded it, and the writing fairly lurched across the page, as though the person gripping the pen had been too excited to fully control her hand.

Lisette did not report on how she had located her rival's cottage. Instead, she plunged directly into a description of the confrontation.

As I suspected, the girl is young, but she is not beautiful. It was obvious to me the instant that I stepped into her cottage that she had used Obeah voodoo to seduce my husband. The hut reeked with the odor of unholy herbs, and seashells lay in small, precise piles at either side of the door. Half-burnt candles stood in a line along the windowsill, and an owl sat sleeping on a perch at the back of the room.

The girl regarded me with eyes that were slanted like a cat's.

I had no need to identify myself, for she recognized me at once.

"Madame Bergé," she said "why are you honoring me with a visit?"

"I think you know that already," I told her stiffly.

"Perhaps I do. I wish, though, that you would tell me yourself."

How I would have loved to have clawed those mocking eyes out! Instead, I spoke with all the dignity I could muster.

"I have come to demand that you cease your affair with my husband."

"I am not inclined to oblige you," the girl said coolly. "It so happens that I have become quite fond of Monsieur Bergé. Not only is he attractive, but he is also extremely generous, and my standard of living has improved since he became my benefactor."

"You have no choice in this matter," I told her. "No matter what spell you may have cast upon him, it cannot begin to rival my own strong claim upon Henri. If my husband loses me, he loses Shadow Grove as well. No sane man would give up his rights to his home and plantation for the likes of you."

The girl regarded me blandly. It was clear that she did not believe me. She was already visualizing herself as the mistress of Shadow Grove.

"It is I, not Henri, who am the owner of Shadow Grove," I informed her. "The house was a gift to me from my parents. If I leave my husband, he will be of no practical use to you. His home and his business are the property of the DuBois family."

"Are they, indeed?" The girl looked thoughtful. She was silent a moment. Her expression did not change, but when she spoke again, I detected a subtle alteration in the tone of her voice. "Perhaps, then, the two of us should strike a bargain. We would neither of us wish for our Henri to become a pauper."

"A bargain!" I scoffed. "What could you own that I would have a use for?" I gestured contemptuously about me at the meager contents of the cottage.

"I am prepared to offer you a fair exchange for your husband's company." She smiled, and her teeth showed small and pointed like those of a river bass. "I have something that you desire greatly, Madame Bergé. I have something for which you have been yearning for quite some time."

"I find that doubtful," I responded. "*You* have something that *I* want? Pray, tell me what is it. The disclosure might amuse me."

"My youth," the girl said simply.

In the silence that followed, the truth of that statement rang out like the clang of a cymbal.

"You are making no sense," I said at last. "You were speaking of barter."

"Can you guess how old I am?" Her cat-eyes were shining.

I did not want to respond, but I could not restrain myself.

"Eighteen?" I hazarded. "Possibly, nineteen?" The smooth skin and firm breasts indicated youth, and yet there was something about her that disconcerted me. "Twenty? What difference does it make? Your youth may have seduced my husband, but it will not hold him prisoner if I wish it to be otherwise."

"I was eighteen when the rites were performed," said the girl. "That was thirty-four years ago."

"That's ridiculous," I exclaimed, but my heart took a sudden leap. Like most Creole children, I was raised on stories of voodoo — of the ceremonies that were said to take place in the swampland — of potions made from snake blood and goat's milk — of sacrifices and offerings. First as a child, and even now, as an adult, I would wake in the night to hear the distant beat of the ritual bata drums and would shiver as I contemplated the magnitude of the dark, strange spells that were being woven at that very moment on the bank of the river.

"What were those rites?" I asked, trying to conceal my eagerness. Was it possible that this woman could be in her *fifties?*

"They were the rites of the Bowl of Years." Her voice was solemn. "Those who drink from the earthen bowl halt the process of aging."

"People grow *younger?*" I whispered in wonder.

"No, that is not possible," said the girl. "Time can be stayed, but it cannot be forced to run backward. I cannot offer youth as you knew it fifteen years ago. What I *can* offer is the chance for you to remain the age you are."

"Are you actually telling me that if I were to take part in this heathen ritual I would never age a day past thirty-five?" I regarded her incredulously. "What would you want from me in return — my immortal soul?"

"What use would I have for your soul?" The girl's strange eyes were bright with amusement. "What I would ask from you would be the support and affection of your husband. Of course, I would not claim him permanently. He would be yours again in good time, when his hair grew gray and his stomach began to sag."

The vision of Henri aging with the years, while I remained untouched by the passage of time, filled me with a surge of malicious satisfaction. Then a sobering thought occurred to me. If I accepted this woman's offer, not only would I witness the aging of Henri, but I would also have to watch the aging of my *children*. I would see my handsome sons become feeble and doddering; I would see my daughter, white-haired and wrinkled, leaning on a cane.

"I could not bear to outlive my children," I said firmly. "My sons and my daughter must also drink from the Bowl of Years."

"Why, most certainly," the girl said readily. "Your children may take part in the rites when you do. They will remain with you always, exactly as they are today."

She averted her eyes, so I could not see the expression there. I am certain, however, that this time they did not contain laughter. Why would any woman laugh at the concept of something so gloriously fulfilling as a mother's having her children with her forever?

CHAPTER

⸻⟨ 17 ⟩⸻

I T was close to six in the morning when I finished reading the final page of Lisette's incredible story, closed the journal, and laid it carefully on the table beside my bed. Then, sinking back upon my pillow, I fell immediately into the deep and dreamless sleep of emotional exhaustion.

When I finally awoke, it was to the sodden heat of midday and to a repeated knock on my bedroom door.

With my eyes still closed, I asked, "Who is it? What do you want?"

Josie's voice spoke through the door.

"Nore, your father wants you downstairs in his study."

"Why?" I asked coldly. "What's he mad about now? Did you tell him I hurt your feelings last night by refusing your escape money?"

"Maman's getting ready to drive him into Baton Rouge to the airport," Josie said, ignoring my sarcasm. "I guess he wants to tell you goodbye."

"To tell me goodbye!" I exclaimed, coming fully awake with a start. "What do you mean 'goodbye'? Where is he going?"

Then, all at once, I remembered something that I had let slip past me, overshadowed as it had been by all the traumatic revelations of the previous day. Dad had said that he had a meeting scheduled with his publisher on Friday. That must mean that this was the day he was flying to New York!

Panic surged through me as I realized the full significance of that fact.

"Tell him I'll be right down!" I cried. "Don't let him leave till I get there!"

Jumping out of bed, I quickly threw on my clothes and rushed out of the bedroom. I was halfway down the hall to the stairs, when the feeling suddenly struck me that I was being watched. I glanced back over my shoulder, taking in the emptiness of the hallway. The door to my bedroom was closed, as was the door to Josie's room. It was possible that the bathroom door might have been standing open a crack, but I could not be sure of this without going back to check on it. There was no time for that now; not if I was going to prevent Dad from deserting me. If people wanted to spy on me, then let them, I told myself. The important thing was that Dad and I leave Shadow Grove together!

When I burst into my father's office, I was relieved to find him alone there, in the process of loading papers into his briefcase.

"So, Sleeping Beauty's awake at last!" he commented when he saw me, red-faced and panting from my dash down the stairs. "Are you sick or something, Nore? You don't usually sleep straight through the morning like this."

"I was tired," I said. "I didn't get much sleep last night."

"I should think that you would have had plenty, considering the hour you must have gone to bed." Dad's voice was devoid of warmth. "I thought you were going to come down and eat dinner with the family."

"I wasn't hungry," I said.

"I don't believe that for one minute. You simply weren't willing to make the apologies I asked of you."

"I'll make them now," I said with feverish eagerness. "I'll apologize to Lisette and to Josie and to you and to Gabe and to anybody else you want me to, but, please, can I go to New York with you, Dad? It's terribly important!"

"Why would you want to do that?" my father asked me. "This isn't going to be a pleasure trip. I'm only going to be in the city for one day, and during that time, I'll be tied up with business meetings."

"That's all right," I said. "We'll still have two evenings together. I need some time alone with you. There are things I need to talk about."

"What sort of things?" Dad asked. "What is there that we can discuss in New York that we can't discuss here?"

"Personal things," I said. "Father-daughter things. The two of us haven't been alone together since Mother died. Is it all that strange that I should want a little time alone with my father?"

"There's not much chance that we could get you a seat on the plane," said Dad. I could see that my mention of Mother had had a softening effect on him. "If you had come up with this suggestion a little bit sooner —"

"At least, we could try!" I said quickly, pressing my advantage. "I could drive you to the airport, and we could check and see how full the plane is. There won't be anything lost if we find out that I can't get a seat. I can either fly standby or just turn around and drive back home."

This last was offered without any belief that it would come to pass. I had no doubt in the world that, after spending an hour and a half alone in the car with me, Dad would reject the idea of either one of us ever returning to Shadow Grove. Now that I had Lisette's journal to confirm my suspicions, I would have no problem in convincing him of the danger we were in.

"What's going on here?" Lisette spoke quietly from the doorway behind me. "Has Nore decided that she wants to ride into Baton Rouge with us?"

"She wants to fly to New York with me," Dad told her. "If there's a seat available, I guess there's no reason why she shouldn't."

"Well, *I* can think of a reason," said Lisette. "After Nore's disgraceful performance yesterday, I don't see how you can even consider treating her to a vacation trip."

"Lis has a point, Nore," said my father. "You certainly haven't earned any special privileges. Your treatment of Josie yesterday was unforgivable."

"I told you that I'd apologize!" I said. I whirled to face Lisette. "I'm sorry I put Josie out of the car! I'm sorry I was rude to you! I'm sorry I accused Gabe —"

"Apologies are well and good," Lisette said coldly, "but they can't erase what took place. This is your daughter, Chuck. I won't try to tell you how to handle her. If you choose to withhold punishment, that's your decision. I do think, though, that it's going a bit too far when you reward her rude behavior with a trip to New York City."

As I saw my father's face beginning to register agreement, my control suddenly disintegrated. In a frenzy of panic, I clutched at Dad's arm.

"Oh, please!" I exclaimed. "You can't go off and leave me

here! You don't know what these people are! You don't know what their plan is!"

"There she goes again," Lisette said with a weary sigh. "She's breaking my heart, Chuck. She can't forgive me for being alive when her own mother isn't, and for falling in love with you and becoming your wife."

"You are *not* in love with my father!" I exploded. "Getting married is your favorite hobby! It's how you get the money to keep Shadow Grove going and to support yourself and your children." I turned frantically to my father. "How many times do you think your wife has been married? Two, right? You think that you're her second husband? Well, you're not! There have been at least six men ahead of you!"

"That's enough, Nore!" Dad said. His voice was shaking with anger. "I've heard all of this that I intend to. After this venomous tirade, there is no way in the world I would consider taking you anywhere."

"But, I've got proof!" I told him. "I've got a whole sheaf of marriage certificates, and there are death certificates too! Just give me a minute, Dad, and I'll run upstairs and get them!"

"I don't want to look at any —" my father began, when Lisette placed a placating hand on his arm.

"It's all right, dear," she said gently. "Can't you see that she's obsessed with this? Please, let her go and get whatever it is that she wants to show you. It's far better to get all these doubts of hers out in the open so they can be explained away."

Dad was silent a moment.

Then he said, "All right, go get this 'proof' of yours, Nore, if you feel you have to, but you'd better make it fast. I have to leave for the airport in five minutes. If you're not back down here by then, forget it."

"Don't worry," I told him, "I'll be back right away."

Shoving past Lisette without acknowledging her existence, I hurried out of the room and up the stairs to the second-floor hallway. As I turned to the right and started down to the east end of the hall, I was confronted by a sight that stopped me dead in my track.

The door to my bedroom was standing open.

"Oh, no!" I whispered, filled with sudden apprehension.

Breaking into a run, I covered the distance to my room in a matter of seconds. When I entered, I found exactly what I had expected. The table, on which I had left the marriage certificates and Lisette's journal, now held nothing but the bedside lamp.

I knew immediately who had taken them. It had to have been Gabe. He had spotted me that morning on my way back from replacing Lisette's keys in her purse and had become suspicious about what I was doing up and about so early. He had undoubtedly been hanging around in the upstairs hallway, waiting for a chance to slip in and investigate my bedroom. It might even have been he, and not my father, who had sent Josie to my door to awaken me with a message guaranteed to send me rushing heedlessly from my room.

My eyes filled with tears of bitterness and frustration. How stupid I had been to have left such important documents unguarded! There was no possibility now of convincing Dad of the truth. After my failure to come back downstairs with the proof that I had promised him, I would never be able to get him to believe me. It was hopeless — and I had no one to blame but myself.

Mother! I screamed silently. Oh, Mother, what can I do?

There was no answer, of course. I'd *had* my answer on my

first day at Shadow Grove. "Repack your things and leave!" my mother had told me. But the message had been lost in a dream, and I had chosen to ignore it. Now, I knew how important it had been, but I knew this too late.

Suddenly, I became aware of the sound of an engine starting up in the driveway. The five minutes that Dad had agreed to give me were up. True to his word, he was preparing to let Lisette drive him to the airport, and for the next day and a half he would be out of my reach.

I would be alone — totally alone — with the Bergés!

Frightened out of my tears by the horrifying prospect, I jumped up from the bed and dashed out onto the balcony. They were taking the Monte Carlo. The engine was running, and Lisette was seated behind the wheel. Dad was standing on the far side, loading his briefcase and overnight bag into the back seat.

"Dad!" I called out to him frantically. "Dad, wait! Please, wait!"

My father turned to glance up at me. Standing there on the balcony with my wild, uncombed hair and frenzied expression, I must have been a sight to behold.

"Please, wait!" I shouted. "I'll be right down! Dad, I've got to go with you!"

"I told you five minutes," Dad called up to me. "It's been almost ten. You know as well as I do that this 'proof' of yours is nonexistent." He paused, and then continued, more gently, "I don't know what your problem is, Nore, but when I get back, we'll tackle it together as a family. We'll go into Merveille for counseling. Lisette says there's a family services agency there. We'll get things worked out, I promise."

"No!" I cried. "No — it can't wait that long! I've got to talk to you now!"

"That's impossible," Dad told me. "I'll be back Saturday

183

evening, and we'll talk then. Meanwhile, behave yourself. I don't want you giving Lisette any problems while I'm gone. Now, I've got to get a move on or I'll miss my plane."

"No!" I cried. "Wait! Please, wait!"

Whirling, I raced from the balcony, through my room, through the hallway and down the stairs. I burst out into the driveway just in time to see the Monte Carlo pulling out through the gate onto the highway. A sudden memory struck me of myself at age three or four, being left with a hated babysitter while my parents went off to a friend's son's bar mitzvah. Screaming and waving, I had chased after them, running straight down the middle of the street in a line of traffic, until my father, catching sight of me in the rearview mirror, had stopped the car, and Mother had run back to get me. "It's all right," she had crooned, gathering me up in her arms. "It's all right, baby. We won't leave you, if it's going to upset you this much."

If I had thought that it would have accomplished that same end, I would have done the identical thing now. I would have run after the car, shrieking "Come back! Come back!" until it stopped or until I dropped from exhaustion. But I was seventeen, not three; and it was Lisette who was driving, not Dad; and my loving, overindulgent mother was not there to rush back for me. There was no way that I could keep my father from leaving. If I was going to be saved, I would have to save myself.

Willing myself to be calm, I tried to get my thoughts into rational enough order so that I could come up with some kind of plan for survival. First and foremost, I knew that I had to escape from Shadow Grove. The danger had been great enough when Dad had been there with me, and my stepfamily had been forced to keep up a facade of normalcy.

This would now no longer be necessary, for they knew that I had discovered everything, and they did not have to pretend to be other than what they were. If my existence had been a threat to them before, it would be a greater one now, especially since Dad had decided on family counseling. In therapy, I would have a chance to tell my story to an authoritative outsider, who would record it in his notes, even if he did not believe it. If days, weeks, or months from then, the famous author Charles Robbins and his daughter were to die as a result of some mysterious accident, there would be someone to rise up and demand an investigation.

If I was not to be brought to the attention of a psychologist, then, I would have to meet with an accident almost immediately. Because of this, I could not risk remaining alone at Shadow Grove at the mercy of the Bergé trio for a moment longer than was absolutely necessary. My father's two-day absence would provide too ideal an opportunity for me to fall down the stairs or take a tumble into the swimming pool.

My one escape hatch — and, thank God, I had one — was Dave Parlange. He was scheduled to pick me up for our "date" at six. Since the Bergés knew nothing about this, they would not be prepared to stop me. I could intercept Dave's car as it pulled through the gate, jump inside and lock the doors, and direct him to drive straight back to Merveille. By the time that Gabe or Lisette could reach their own car and start to follow us, we would be gone.

The knowledge that Dave would be coming did a lot to calm me. All I had to do was to hold out for another four hours. During that time, however, I would have to conceal myself. Although Lisette was not there at the moment, Gabe and Josie still had to be reckoned with, and their combined forces represented a considerable threat. Would they, I wondered, expect me to reenter the house? Could they really believe that I would be that stupid? Yes, possibly they could, for I had not proved myself too bright with some of the other, less-than-clever moves that I had made recently. My guess was that, at that very moment, they were gazing down at me through the half-open louvers of their balcony doors, waiting to see if they would have to come after me or if I would come to them.

Well, at least, this offered me a way to gain some time for myself. Painfully conscious that two pairs of eyes were probably observing me, I turned and walked slowly back toward the house, as though intending to enter. Once I had mounted the porch steps and was safely out of sight of anyone who might be looking down from above, I ran down the length of the porch, climbed over the railing, and dropped to the ground at its far east end.

Sticking close to the side of the house, I walked swiftly toward the back, glancing about for some place in which to conceal myself. The estate was so large that it offered numerous possibilities — heavy growths of bushes, clumps of blossoming trees, sheds, storage areas, the dovecotes, the remains of the deteriorating stable. Where, I asked myself frantically, would Gabe and Josie be least inclined to come searching?

Glancing past the line of slave cabins, my eyes came to rest on the tiny, private cemetery. It sat, fully exposed, just beyond the row of slave cabins, so visible to the eye that it hardly seemed to qualify as a possible hiding place. At the same time, it was so overgrown that it was almost a thicket of greenery, and the rounded tops of the tombstones could barely be seen above waist-high weeds.

It was ironic, I thought, that the two deceased members of this family were destined to offer me refuge from the three who were still living. Leaving the shelter of the wall, I broke into a run, cleared the stretch of ground that separated me from the miniature graveyard, and plunged through the narrow opening in the wrought-iron fence. Brambles tore at my legs, and a swarm of gnats rose in a humming cloud from a clump of daisies. Dropping down between the two tombstones, I made a nest for myself in the thick, damp grass and settled there for a long and miserable wait.

CHAPTER

18

THE hours passed slowly.

To keep my mind occupied, I played a game with myself in which I tried to recall the happenings of each year of my life. The earliest of these years were, of course, devoid of memories, but the year that I had turned three held the memory of a teddy bear named Sam and a ride on a merry-go-round. The summer that I was four, my parents had rented a cottage at the New Jersey shore, and I could recall a strip of white beach and a moat-encircled sandcastle with a seagull feather stuck on top, and a wave that had knocked me down and filled me with terror. When I was five, I had started kindergarten, and my teacher had let me clean the blackboard, and a little boy named Michael had made me a Valentine.

I had worked my way up to my eighth year and was in the process of steering my mental way through that, when I heard Josie's voice calling, "Nore! Nore, where are you?"

Huddling lower in my hollow between the tombstones, I fought back panic and stubbornly kept my mind riveted to its appointed task.

Eight years old — a case of chicken pox — a red bicycle with training wheels — my first overnight at the house of a friend name Heather. Nine years old — my father had signed me up to take swimming lessons at the YWCA, but I had refused to go. I was petrified at the thought of getting my head under water.

"Nore! There's something important I need to tell you! Nore, where are you? Please, come back to the house so we can talk!"

At the age of ten I had discovered the joys of reading. My mother had dragged down from the attic a box of treasured volumes that she had saved from her own childhood, and we had spent months poring over its contents. Together we had mourned the death of sweet Beth in *Little Women,* and had accompanied Nancy Drew on her wild adventures. We had chanted together the poetry of Vachel Lindsay, and giggled over the tongue-in-cheek humor of Dorothy Parker.

Eleven years old — and twelve — and, then, at long last, I'd celebrated the landmark occasion of my thirteenth birthday. I could remember getting up that morning and heading straight for the mirror. Despite the fact that the face that looked back at me now belonged to a teenager, it had undergone no miraculous transformation. The cheeks were still too babyishly round, the features too undefined; the aura of glamour and sophistication that I had hoped to find there was still sadly lacking. The only difference in my appearance involved my chin, which overnight had blossomed out in a cluster of pimples. I let out a wail of horror that shook the house.

Determinedly keeping my mind dredging up memories, I refused to let it take focus on the present. I knew that if that were to happen, I could easily give way to terror. Although Josie's voice was no longer calling my name, it was obvious that she had not given up on finding me. Every once in a while, as I peered out through the screen of tall grass that concealed me, I caught a glimpse of her bright yellow T-shirt as she came popping unexpectedly around the corner of the house or traversed the path that led to the lily pond. As for Gabe — I had no idea where he might be. I could only guess that he was out there searching for me also.

I returned to my game, my instrument of self-preservation. At thirteen years old, I had suddenly declared war on my parents. Instead of my closest friends, they had abruptly become "the enemy," out to wreck my life with their unreasonable regulations. Everything that I wanted to do seemed to be forbidden. I could not stay out past eleven; I could not go to rock concerts; I could not attend mixed parties, unless there were adult chaperones. The one occasion on which I cut class to go with some friends to an afternoon movie, I was hauled out of my theater seat by my father, who had been in his home office at the typewriter when the attendance office called. (All of my friends had *normal* parents who worked outside of the home.)

It was a horrendous year for all of us, but I did move past it. My fourteenth year and my fifteenth year were better. I outgrew my training bra and my adolescent acne and was finally given permission to start single dating. The face in my bathroom mirror began to smile back at me, and my parents seemed suddenly not as bad as I'd thought they were. Unlike Josie, held forever — a bud that would never bloom — I moved gratefully out of that no-man's-land of just-past-childhood.

I carried my remembrance game through to the beginning of my sixteenth year and then discontinued it. I refused to relive the pain of my mother's death.

At ten past five, I heard the sound of Lisette's car pulling into the driveway. I was not situated so that I could actually see it, but I recognized the pitch of the engine of the Monte Carlo. It drew to a stop in front of the house, and a car door opened and slammed shut. A few moments later, I heard the front screen door to the house bang closed.

Now, instead of counting bygone years, I began to count current minutes, as the hour of six became increasingly more imminent. Twenty minutes to go — now fifteen — now ten! I knew that I had to be positioned at the end of the driveway in order to intercept Dave before he could continue on up to the house. The only way that I could think of to get down there was to stay close to the line of oaks that bordered the drive. The sun was low enough now so that the trees threw dark pools of shade onto the lawn to the east. If I worked my way down the row, darting from shadow pocket to shadow pocket, there was a chance that I could make the journey undetected.

Hauling myself stiffly to my feet, I peered cautiously about me. I could see no sign of life in any direction. Was it possible, I wondered, that all the members of the Bergé family were gathered inside the house, discussing my whereabouts? Hoping desperately that this was the case, I left the sanctuary of the tiny graveyard and ran swiftly across the open expanse of lawn that separated the cemetery from the driveway. Plunging into the shadow of the nearest of the oak trees, I pressed myself close against the huge trunk and turned to focus my eyes on the end of the drive. With a sense of shock, I saw that, for the first time since my arrival at Shadow Grove, the great iron gate was closed and padlocked.

191

It was all that I could do to keep from bursting into tears. I could not believe that I had been so easily outmaneuvered! With the driveway sealed, there would be no way that Dave could get in to rescue me. I would be trapped, alone and defenseless, at the mercy of the Bergé trio until my father got back from his trip.

Struggling to keep from giving way to despair, I tried to force my mind into more positive thinking. I must not allow myself to be numbed by panic. If I could not get out through the gate, then I would have to find another route to safety. Perhaps, I thought, I might be able to get over the fence. The wrought-iron fence ran all the way around the estate, and at some point along the way, there had to be some means of scaling it. In fact, if I remembered correctly, one of the dovecotes out by the stables stood adjacent to it. If I climbed that, I might be able to scramble over the top of the fence and drop to the ground on its far side. Then I could circle back to the highway and meet Dave at the outside of the gate.

Without permitting myself to dwell upon the danger of further exposure, I left the shelter of the oak tree and fled back across the lawn in the direction from which I had come. Half expecting at any moment to hear Josie call out my name or to see Lisette emerge from the entrance to the patio, I bypassed the cemetery and continued on toward the back of the house.

As I came opposite the slave cabins, a thought occurred to me that caused me to pause in my flight for a moment of reflection. If I did escape from Shadow Grove and told Dave all the things I'd discovered, he would be no more likely to believe them than my father had been. The tale of the Bergé family was so incredible that no one could reasonably be expected to accept it without evidence. If I was to entertain any hope of convincing anyone of the truth of my story, I would have to back it up with something concrete.

The evidence I needed lay in the storage cabin. Although I was no longer in possession of Lisette's diary, there were other documents and photographs that could serve to substantiate the family history. They were probably all still there — there hadn't been time yet for their removal — but once Lisette came to realize I was gone, they would be whisked away quickly.

Much as I dreaded the thought of delaying escape, I could see no alternative — I had to grab some documents. Reversing direction, I headed for the cabin. When I reached it, I was relieved to discover that the lock was still positioned as I had left it, with the pivoted shackle inserted through, but not shoved closed upon, the ring in the door.

I plucked the padlock free, hastily pulled the door open, and stepped inside. Then, as I stretched out my hand for the light switch, I suddenly froze. Instinctively, I knew that I was not the only occupant of the room. Someone else was there in the darkness with me.

For a moment I stood unmoving, weighing my options. They were dismayingly few. I could whirl and rush back out through the open doorway, but there was nowhere to go from there. Whoever it was who was waiting for me in the room's black interior obviously had an accomplice. Someone else had to have replaced the lock on the outside of the door so that I would be tricked into believing that it had not been tampered with. This second person would now be positioned to intercept me if I took flight. Whether I fled or whether I stayed, escape was impossible.

Bracing myself, I groped for the switch and flicked on the light.

My companion in the storeroom was Gabe Bergé.

"So, it's you!" I was so swept with anger that my fear was momentarily minimized. "It's good old Gabe, the guy who's so ready to fall in love with me! What are you doing here in the dark like a snake in a bush? Were you hoping to finish up the job you flubbed on the river?"

"I can't blame you for being bitter, Nore," Gabe said quietly. "If you'll be fair, though, you'll have to admit that I offered you an out."

"The chance to run away with you?" I exclaimed sarcastically. "What sort of an 'out' was that? While you and I were in California, my father would have been left at the mercy of your mother. That black widow spider would have finished him off in a day!"

"You're wrong about that," Gabe said. "With you gone, he would have been perfectly safe here. You and my mother are both named in his will. On your father's death, his estate is to be divided equally between the two of you. For Maman to inherit it all, Chuck will have to outlive you."

He uttered this statement so matter-of-factly that for a moment I was as unaffected by it as I would have been if he had told me that his family was holding off on buying a television set until there was a sale. Then the full meaning of what he had said came through to me, and I regarded him incredulously.

"You mean Lisette studies the wills of her husbands as though they were *contracts!* She gets rid of the competition and then goes for the jackpot!"

"What choice does she have?" Gabe asked me reasonably. "That's the only way we can survive. We have to live by a different set of standards from those of other people. You can't get a job without having a Social Security number, and to get that, you have to show a birth certificate. That, of course, is something that none of our family can do."

"But to kill people off!"

"We all of us hate that part of it," said Gabe. "If Maman had her way, she'd wait out her husbands' natural lifetimes. The problem is that she can't remain married to anyone long enough for him to notice that none of us is aging. We can't even live here at Shadow Grove for more than a couple of years at a time, or the people in Merveille might start noticing that we're different. We have to go off to some big city and get lost in the crowds for a while. Then we come back and pass ourselves off as a new generation."

"No matter how sensible you try to make it sound, what you're talking about is *murder,*" I said. "Your mother is a monster. I can't believe that you and Josie love her."

"We *have* to love her," Gabe said. "She's the one who takes care of us. There's no way that Jo or I could make it on our own. Back in earlier times, I could sometimes take off by myself for a while. Around nineteen hundred, for instance, when I was with Felicité, the two of us built a cabin. She had a garden, and I fished the river, until she grew past me. Then she got married to some farmer, and I came back home. Life today has become too complicated for that sort of arrangement. Without a birth certificate, you can't even get a driver's license. That's why Maman drives like a snail and never takes chances."

"Well, that explains something," I said. "It's no wonder you couldn't afford to be arrested. And to think that I was crazy enough to take the blame that night!"

"Try not to hate us, Nore," Gabe said imploringly. He took an impulsive step toward me. Automatically, I stepped back away from him, and then wished that I hadn't. Up until then, I had been standing in front of the doorway, but now Gabe was blocking it, which cut off my only access to the outside world.

"We're locked into something we can't get out of," Gabe continued. "Maman was impulsive and didn't think things through. She didn't fully understand what it was she was getting us into. If she had, you can bet that she'd never have made her deal. She's the one to be pitied, not the men she marries. They get to move on to whatever God has planned for them. Maman's stuck here forever, 'raising' kids who will never be grown. Jo and I are her responsibility for all of eternity."

"I'm not sorry for her," I said. "She's a horrible person. And you — you're just as terrible — maybe even more so. You pretended you cared about me and then tried to drown me."

"I didn't 'pretend,' " Gabe objected. "I really do care about you. I have no choice. I have to do what Maman tells me. Back when Louis was alive, it was he who —"

What happened next was sudden. It occured so abruptly, in fact, that I had not the slightest indication that anything was coming. One moment Gabe was standing with his back to the doorway, and the next, he was flying forward across the room. He crashed full-tilt into the far wall and then stumbled backward, struggling desperately to regain his balance. Then his legs seemed to buckle, and he crumpled to the floor, landing hard on his knees.

"Don't get up until I say so, or you're going to get flattened." Dave Parlange's broad shoulders seemed to fill the doorway completely. "This is one time I don't plan to show respect for my 'elders.' " He turned his attention to me. "Are you okay, Nore? Did that creep hurt you?"

I shook my head, too stunned by surprise at his unexpected arrival to bring forth an answer.

"When I saw the gate was locked, I figured that something was wrong," Dave said. "I climbed up on the roof of my car and dropped over the fence." He stepped into the room and glanced about with interest. "Well, I see old Charlie was right. There's tons of stuff here. Were you able to find the information you wanted?"

"Yes," I told him shakily, regaining control of my voice. "Lisette kept a diary that spelled out everything. I tried to tell Dad about it, but he wouldn't believe me. He left today on a business trip, and he won't be back until Saturday. I was scared that I wouldn't be alive when he returned."

"After overhearing our friend here, I doubt that you would have been," Dave said. He turned to Gabe. "I want you to give me the key to the gate."

"I don't have it," Gabe said. "Nore can tell you that my mother carries all the keys. There's no way that you'll ever get out of here unless she wants you to."

"I wouldn't count on that," said Dave. "I got myself *in,* you know." He crossed to Gabe and bent to grab hold of his wrist. "Get up and go get that key. I know you can if you want to."

"I don't give orders to Maman," Gabe said. "She's the one who makes the rules." Nevertheless, he did as directed and struggled to his feet. He grimaced as Dave gripped his arm and bent it behind him.

"Come on with us, Nore," Dave said. "Either we'll get that key from your stepmother, or I'll hoist you over the fence and we'll get out that way."

So the three of us left the storeroom and walked out through the open doorway into the gentle beauty of the deepening twilight.

Lisette stood quietly waiting there with a gun.

CHAPTER

⸻⸪⟨ 19 ⟩⸪⸻

LISETTE looked so *young*.

Even knowing what I did — or, perhaps, *because* I knew what I did — my first reaction upon seeing her there, standing against the hedge behind the patio, was that she looked more like a child than a full-grown woman. She was wearing a simple, white sundress, cinched tight at the waist, and her slim, bare arms had a vulnerable, unmuscled softness. Her hair was not pinned up, as she often wore it, but fell loose about her shoulders in a thick, dark cloud. The fragile perfection of her features was emphasized by the freshness of her skin. Her cheeks were softly flushed, and her eyes were wide and lovely.

I had never seen her so beautiful. Or so terrifying.

The long-barreled, pearl-handled pistol that she gripped in both her hands was one of the antique firearms from the gun case in the parlor.

"Release my son, please, Mr. Parlange," Lisette said

quietly. "A former husband of mine was an expert with firearms. He taught me to shoot, and although it's been some time since I've done so, it would be very unlikely that I would miss at this close range."

I could see by Dave's face that he didn't know how seriously to take this.

"You wouldn't take the chance of hitting Gabe," he said.

"No, I wouldn't," Lisette agreed. "But, then, I wouldn't have to. Nore is exposed and has no one to use as a shield. I think you would be wise to let Gabriel go."

Dave glanced across at me, and his bravado deserted him. He released his grip on Gabe's wrist, and Gabe stepped quickly away and moved to his mother's side.

"You told me that you could handle this on your own," Lisette said accusingly. "It's a lucky thing I decided to keep an eye on things."

"I wanted a chance to talk to Nore alone," Gabe said. "She'd found out so much that I thought she should hear the rest. There wouldn't have been any problems if Josie's pal, here, hadn't come bursting in on us the way he did."

"I was out on the balcony and saw him come over the fence," said Lisette. "I couldn't imagine who he was or what he was doing here." She turned to Dave. "What *are* you doing here, Mr. Parlange? Surely you know by now that Celina no longer works here."

"He didn't come to see Celina," said Gabe. "He came to see Nore. He's had his eye on her ever since that night at the disco. He asked her then if —"

He left the sentence fall away, uncompleted, obviously realizing that he had already said too much.

"What night at the disco?" Lisette responded immediately. There was an edge to her voice. "I don't recall that I gave permission for any such excursion. In fact, I distinctly remember vetoing that idea."

"Stop talking to me as though I were a child, Maman," Gabe said. "You should know that I've been around for a while. If I'm not able to make a few decisions on my own by this time, then I never will be."

"That's the point I was trying to make, dear," Lisette said calmly. "You will never be able to make mature decisions. You will always be mentally and emotionally a boy. I should have hoped that you would have benefited from your brother's tragic example. Louis never would have had his accident if he had obeyed me when I told him he wasn't to ride that stallion."

"What happened to Louis was no accident," Gabe said bitterly.

"What do you mean by that statement?"

"Lou knew that he wasn't strong enough to control that horse," said Gabe. "He knew the risk he was taking if he tried to jump it. He took that risk because he wanted to — because he was tempting fate — because he was sick of living the way we have to live. Louis hated the things you made him do. He hated his dependency. He thought that sixty-nine years of childhood was enough."

"I know you don't believe that," Lisette said with a nervous laugh. "You're saying it only in a childish attempt to hurt me. Well, it isn't going to work, dear, because I know what lies behind these little flareups of yours. You've allowed yourself to get too attached to a girl again. That always results in your getting upset and bitter."

"If he's 'attached' to Nore, he's sure picked an odd way of showing it," said Dave. "What do you two have planned for us now — another little boat ride?"

"No, you're going back into the cabin," Lisette informed

him. "Gabe, go get the keys out of the purse in my bedroom and bring the car around to the front of the house. You and Josie wait for me there. I'll be joining you shortly."

Gabe turned to me. "Nore, I'm sorry. I'm not responsible."

"You *are* responsible," I shot back. "You're Maman's Little Henchman. It makes me sick to realize that I once thought I might be in love with you."

That would have made a great parting line if my eyes had not betrayed me by suddenly filling up with uncontrollable tears.

"Into the cabin, Nore," my stepmother ordered. Could that possibly be a note of regret that I heard in her voice? There flashed through my mind the memory of our conversation in the kitchen on the morning that she had sent me to meet Gabe by the river. "I wish your relationship with us were different," she had told me then.

At the time, of course, I had not understood her meaning. Whatever measure of affection she felt for me — if, indeed, she did feel any — was clearly not sufficient to keep her from following whatever plan she had made. The pistol in her hands did not waver. She nodded toward the cabin, and I knew that I had no alternative but to enter it.

Once ensconced in the storage room, out of the sight of Gabe and his mother, I covered my face with my hands and let the tears come. I wept for myself, of course — and for Dave, whom I had dragged into this mess — and for my father, so blinded by infatuation that he was not aware of danger. And I wept for Gabe — yes, even for Gabe — for in that one final instant before I had turned away, I had looked into his face and seen there such pain and hopelessness that I could not bring myself to truly hate him.

I heard the sound of Dave's footsteps entering the cabin

and then the thud of the door slamming closed. Then there was the metallic clink of the padlock being snapped into place. A moment later, I felt a hand on my shoulder. Dave turned me toward him, and, sobbing, I threw myself into his arms.

"Don't cry," he said gruffly as he cradled me against his chest. "The crazy lady's gone now. You and I are safe in here. We'll just hole up for a while until your dad gets back."

"Dad won't be back for two whole days!" I wailed.

"So, it's not the end of the world if we wait two days," Dave said. "Our stomachs may growl, but at least we'll have plenty to read."

His attempt to make light of such a miserable situation both touched and angered me.

"You don't understand," I said, pulling back so that I could look up at him. "You don't really think this is all there is to it, do you? Lisette isn't going to walk off and leave us to be rescued. We know too much for her to allow that. We'd wreck everything for her."

"Then why didn't she shoot us while we were out in the yard?" Dave asked me reasonably. "She had the opportunity, and she didn't use it. You heard her send Gabe to get his sister and bring the car around. The family's going away, and they're obviously not taking us with them, so I don't really see what we have to worry about."

"Lisette didn't want to shoot us if she could help it," I said. "Bullets in people are hard to pass off as accidents. That doesn't mean, though, that she doesn't have other plans for us. She can't afford to let us out of here alive."

"We'll see about that," said Dave. "There's no way she can get the jump on us now. She and Gabe can't get the lock off that door without our hearing them. If I'm prepared and standing ready, I can swing a pretty heavy fist. Nobody who steps through that doorway will get very far."

"We can turn off the light," I said, beginning to feel more hopeful. "They won't be able to see you if they're stepping into darkness."

"And you can distract them by making some noise at the side of the room," Dave said. "They'll turn their heads in that direction, and — *wham!* — they've had it." He pulled me back against him and gave me a hug. "I don't have a handkerchief, but you can wipe your eyes on my shirt."

"I appreciate the offer, but I have a shirt of my own," I told him. It was comforting just to stand there, encircled by his arms. "Can you imagine what it would be like to know that you were never going to grow old? That, if you took perfect care of yourself and never had an accident, you might be able to live till the end of the world?"

"It sounds pretty boring to me," said Dave. "It would be like playing a record and having the needle get stuck in a groove." He tightened his arms in one final squeeze and then released me. "Well, where do we start our reading? Is this stuff in any sort of order? That journal you were talking about — "

"Dave," I interrupted, "I smell gasoline."

"You smell *what?*" He regarded me with surprise. "There's nothing like that in here. It must be those papers and things you smell. When paper gets old and musty —" He broke off in midsentence and sniffed at the air. "No — wait — you're right. I can smell it too. It *does* smell like gas."

"There!" I cried. "Look!"

I pointed to the far corner of the room where a curl of gray smoke was rising lazily toward the ceiling. Stiff with shock, I stood immobilized, with my hand suspended in air, watching the wisp fan out and begin to expand in all directions.

"She must have taken the fuel can Gabe uses for the outboard," I said to Dave, too stunned to feel anything yet but numbness. "She's doused the side of the cabin and ignited the gas. What she's planning to do is to burn us alive in here."

"That's impossible," said Dave. "Not even Lisette would do that."

Then he turned to stare in the direction that I was pointing. The entire corner of the storeroom was now rapidly misting with smoke, and my eyes were already beginning to smart from the fumes. In the silence that had fallen upon us, I became aware of a crackling sound that had previously been covered by our voices.

I knew what that sound must mean, and a scream started building at the back of my throat.

"This cabin's a tinderbox," Dave said in strange, flat voice, as though he could not quite grasp the meaning of what he was saying. "As old and as dry as the wood is, it'll go up like a bonfire."

As if on cue, a thin tongue of flame came darting in through the crack between two widely spaced boards and began to lick hungrily at the inside surface of the wall.

Instinctively, I started to back away from it. Then, regaining control of my senses, I reversed direction and rushed toward it instead. Squinting my eyes half closed against the smoke, I began to kick the nearby piles of papers and documents back out of reach of the flame. Once those papers ignited, fire would sweep from stack to stack, and in seconds the interior of the room would be engulfed in flames.

"I'm going to see if I can break down the door," Dave said.

I nodded without speaking, knowing that if I once allowed my lips to part, I would be lost in a helpless state of hysteria.

Pressing my hands to my mouth, I watched as Dave backed away from the door and gathered himself for the charge. Then, like a football lineman, he went hurtling forward. His shoulder crashed into the door with so much force that it seemed impossible that the aged boards would not shatter. When he stepped back, however, I saw that the wood was stronger than it looked. The door had held, and the hinges were still set in place.

Dave readied himself for a second charge. This time, I shut my eyes, unable to allow myself to watch any further. The room was growing dense with smoke, and every breath I took caused me to break into a new round of coughing. The initial crackling sound had by now become a steady roar, and the heat from the wall behind me was becoming intense. There was one heavy thud — and then another — and still another, as Dave hurled himself again and again against the door.

"Get down on the floor!" he yelled at me. "The smoke won't be so heavy there!"

I did as commanded, doubled over in a fit of coughing. There was another crash, and I heard Dave give a strangled sob, which was the most terrifying sound that I had heard so far, for it was an indication of the hopelessness of our situation.

Then, suddenly, I sensed the fact that something new was happening. Blinded by smoke, I could not tell at first exactly what it was. Then I felt the movement of air against my face and forced open my eyes. Through the wall of haze, I saw to my disbelief that the door to the cabin was now standing open.

Frantically, I began to drag myself across the floor in the direction of freedom. Every inch I covered seemed like a mile. The heat at my back was like a furnace, fanned as the flames now were by the sudden intake of air. Dizziness struck me, and I lost all sense of reality. I could no longer raise my head to see where I was going. Still, I kept inching my way forward on my hands and knees, spurred by the knowledge that my final chance for survival was to reach that doorway.

"Nore!" someone called to me. "Nore! Not that way — *this way!*"

I couldn't tell from which direction the words were coming.

Hands slid under my armpits and I felt myself being lifted and half carried, half dragged, across the rough-hewn boards of the floor. Then, before I could take in what was happening, heavenly coolness washed over my face. Incredibly, I was out of doors, lying in the sweet, damp grass, choking and gasping as I dragged in great gulps of clear, clean air.

"Are you okay?" an anxious young voice asked me. "I got you out in time? You didn't get burned?"

Unable to speak, I managed to force open my eyes. Josie's worried face hung suspended above me.

"Are you okay, Nore?" she asked again. Her eyes were huge and frightened.

"Dave!" I managed to gasp. "Dave — is he still in there?"

"I'm safe, Nore," Dave's voice said. "We both got out, and none too soon."

His face appeared above me next to Josie's. Beyond their heads, I could see an inferno of bright orange flames leaping skyward in a great surging fountain of deadly light.

"How did you do it?" I whispered to Josie. "How did you get us out? If Dave couldn't force the door, then how could *you?*"

"Gabe gave me the key," she told me. "He got it off Maman's ring. He told me he and Maman were driving to Merveille to get the fire department. He said the moment they pulled out of the drive, I was to let you out."

"Your mother will be furious," I said. "When she and Gabe get back —"

"They're not coming back," said Josie. "Maman was tired of me. No mother should have to take care of her kids forever."

Her voice was small and tremulous.

"That's not why she left, Jo," Dave said gently. "I'm sure that she and Gabe *did* go into town to get the fire department. There's no phone here to call from, and your mother doesn't want Shadow Grove to burn to the ground. And I'm certain, too, that she *is* coming back. She would never walk out on you. Her love for her children is the strongest, most positive force in her life."

"They're *not* coming back," said Josie. "I know, because when Gabe left, he kissed me goodbye. He's never kissed me before, not even on my birthday. Guys don't do that to their sisters, just to their girlfriends."

"He never kissed me either," I told her softly. "But, then, I guess I was never exactly a girlfriend."

Josie started to cry then in earnest.

And so did I.

That was last summer.

It is winter now.

Summer comes late in New England, but winter comes early. Beyond my dorm room window, a heavy bank of snowclouds coats the silver-gray of the December sky. The first semester of my senior year is almost over.

This past weekend I was Dave's date for a party at Harvard, and in another week, I will be flying to Guilderland for Christmas. Thanks to the fact that there was little wind on the day of the fire at Shadow Grove, the main house escaped the flames that ravished the slave quarters. The whole estate was recently purchased by the state of Louisiana to be converted into a historical museum. The money from the sale has been placed in a trust fund for Josie, and "home" for us now is once again Dad's and my house in New York state.

Poor Dad! To lose two wives in two years would be a shattering experience for any man, but my father has borne his second loss better than his first one.

"I loved Lis, Nore," he told me the day of the funeral. "Sometimes though, I had an odd feeling that I didn't really know her. Even at those moments when we should have been closest, I would find myself wondering what it was she was really thinking and feeling. If we could only have had more time, we might have grown as close as your mother and I were. Lis was so young — so beautiful —"

His voice broke, and I put my arms around him.

"She *was* beautiful, Dad," I said in gentle agreement. I closed my eyes and in memory felt the brush of cool lips against my cheek and inhaled once again the faint, light scent of gardenias.

I have not told my father what happened on that last day at Shadow Grove. He could not handle that knowledge right now, even if he were to believe me. It seems enough for him simply to know that Gabe, with Lisette in the seat beside him, missed a curve in the road on his high-speed trip into Merveille. According to police, the force with which the Monte Carlo struck the mammoth tree killed both its occupants instantly. The realization that Lisette and her son did not suffer gives Dad some measure of comfort, and the knowledge that he is responsible for raising Lisette's young daughter provides him with a sense of purpose.

"You will be on your own soon, Nore," he tells me. "Josie will still have need of me for years."

I try not to smile at the irony of that statement. The time will come, of course, when he will have to know the truth. Perhaps, as years go by, he will begin to become aware of it on his own, or perhaps it will fall to Josie or me to tell him.

The truth must also be handed down to my children, which is why I am putting this incredible story on paper. Lisette's journal is gone, and it must be replaced with my own. By the time that my future children are old enough to read this, they may already have noticed that their "Aunt Josie" is not like other people. It is likely that they will accept this fact without question, for she will have been a part of their lives for as long as they can remember, first in their grandfather's home and then in our own. Her face will be as familiar

209

to them as mine is — perhaps even more familiar — for hers will be a constant, and mine will be subtly changing with the years.

Eventually, it will be their turn to serve as Josie's parents. I hope they will love her enough to be patient with her adolescent moodiness. It is strange to think that Josie may be babysitting my great-great-grandchildren many years after I have departed from this earth.